Billy
and the
EPIC
Escape

Jamie Oliver

Illustrated by Mónica Armiño

PUFFIN

Contents

Billy
and the
EPIC
Escape

This is for all the kids out there who
struggle with their confidence and
doubt themselves, just like Billy –
I believe in you, and the Rhythm does,
too. Find your tribe, and look after
each other, just like Billy, Anna, Jimmy
and Andy, and Grandad, too.

Prologue

'**D**ad, Dad, is it time to go back to Waterfall Woods?' Autumn asked me, as she and her twin brother, Jesse, got ready for bed. It had been just over a week since our last bedtime story about my adventures as a kid, and Autumn and Jesse had been pleading with me almost every night to tell them what happened next.

'All right, all right!' I said. 'In fact, seeing as it's the first night of your summer holidays, it might be the perfect time, because that's when the next part of the story happened, too.'

'HURRAY!' the kids cheered, dancing around the bedroom.

It was a warm summer's evening, and the window was open, letting in an orange sunset glow. With every gentle gust of wind the smell of a different dinner wafted in, and the chirping sound of birds floated above the usual traffic and sirens. The world was slowly winding down; it was the perfect moment for a new bedtime story.

'Now, where did we leave off?' I started, as the twins scrambled into bed.

Before I could say anything else, Autumn pressed her finger to my lips. 'NO, Dad! Let me get us up to date,' she said with a grin. 'I haven't stopped thinking about Waterfall Woods since you finished the last story! SO. Billy – that's you, Dad! – Jimmy, Andy and Anna –'

'You mean Mum!' interrupted Jesse.

'That's right,' Autumn said, nodding. 'But shush, Jesse, I'm telling this story! So, waaaaay back in the 1800s . . .'

I chuckled. 'You mean the 1980s – don't be cheeky.'

'In the *1980s*,' Autumn began again. 'You and your friends discovered a magical windowy thing near your village that took you into the special world of Waterfall Woods.'

'Because you hugged the tree!' piped up Jesse again. Autumn gave him a stern look, but he just stuck his tongue out at her.

'Anyway,' Autumn continued. 'Waterfall Woods was full of creatures like Sprites and Boonas and GIANTS, and it needed your help! Basil and Chief Mirren and all the Sprites were in danger because the Rhythm had gone funny. Remember the Rhythm? It's the heartbeat of the forest, but it's not like one thing, it's everything!'

'Yeah, everything is connected,' added Jesse. 'Everyone has to do their bit, or the Rhythm can't work properly.'

'That's right,' I said, impressed that so much had stayed with them. Just a few weeks ago,

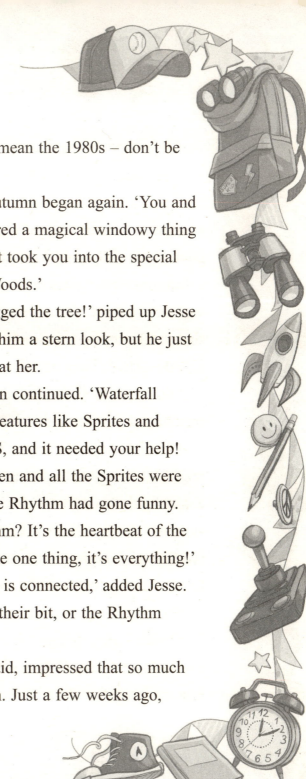

reading a story at bedtime was the last thing Autumn ever wanted to do, because, like me, she found it really difficult. So I felt a warm glow seeing her face light up as she recounted my tale back to me. I'd wanted her and Jesse to understand that stories come in all forms and were much more about imagination and wonder than getting every word right. And it seemed like it had worked. They were hooked!

'You found a farm that was polluting the river and helped put that right to rebalance the Rhythm,' Autumn went on. 'Then you discovered a GIANT in a garden, except it turned out that Bilfred didn't start out as a Giant – he just ate amazing things and grew humongous – and he was actually the long-lost brother of an old man in your village called Wilfred Revel. The brothers were reunited so everyone could live happily ever after,' she said proudly.

'Well, reuniting Wilfred and Bilfred was really just the start,' I told her. 'And you might have to wait a bit longer for the happily-ever-after . . .'

Jesse jumped on to Autumn's bed and both kids snuggled down under the covers.

'You'd better get started, then, Dad!' Autumn said. 'And don't forget all the juicy details!'

'Yes! We want THEM ALL!' Jesse shouted.

I nudged them over so I could sit down on the bed. 'Some of the next part of the story might seem unbelievable, but I promise you it's all true. AND SECRET! You have to promise you won't tell a soul – this is just ours. We have to protect Waterfall Woods,' I said, putting out my little finger for them to link with theirs. 'Twinky promise?'

The kids started to put out theirs when Jesse suddenly realized something. 'What, we *still* have to protect it? Are Basil and the others *still* there?'

'We'll get to that . . .' I said with a wink. 'So can I trust you?'

'YES! Twinky promise,' they chorused.

'Right, let's begin . . .'

Chapter 1

Jimmy Is Eleven!

Billy was sure this was going to be the BEST SUMMER EVER.

It had been six weeks since the incredible adventure in Waterfall Woods with his best friends, Anna, Jimmy and Andy. Since then, they'd been sneaking back into the woods whenever they could to visit Wilfred and Bilfred Revel and the Sprites. But the run-up to the end of term had been chaotic with sports days, awards nights, end-of-term performances and the dreaded parents' evening. Again.

Now, school had FINALLY finished, and a whole six weeks of freedom stretched ahead of them. The friends had big plans!

Billy had persuaded Anna to give him some climbing lessons so he could scamper up rocks as quickly as she could. Jimmy had set himself a summer project of growing his unofficial home zoo to include over 325 different animals. Meanwhile, Andy was determined to get the Guinness World Record for making the biggest elastic band or tinfoil ball, whichever came first.

But these weren't the only ideas they wanted to put into action over the summer. There were still LOADS of mysteries in the woods to uncover. Like working out where the mysterious map they had started putting together led, and finding out if there really were more Giants like Bilfred. And they still didn't know who really owned the flying buzzpacks they'd been using to zip around the woods.

With lots still to find out, the best friends had spent the last few weeks getting plans in place to make sure that they would be able to stay out all day and even overnight without their parents worrying or suspecting that they were running riot in a magical world.

Their usual 'Operation Overnight' strategy of calling to say they were at each other's houses wasn't going to help if they were all in the woods, so they had come up with a genius plan. Anna had seen an advert for a kids' holiday club nearby, so they'd all convinced their parents to pay and sign them up, giving them loads of time to investigate the woods. And Jimmy had come up with the idea of recording messages on his cassette player in case they did need to stay with the Sprites overnight. All they had needed was someone willing to play the messages over the phone to their parents, and Andy had lent Johnny Perks from their class at school his whole stash of *Beano* comics for the summer in exchange for making the calls.

Each of them had recorded a few different excuses on tape and had agreed with Johnny that if he didn't hear from one of them by 6 p.m., he would set the plan in motion. It was foolproof!

But, at least for today, Waterfall Woods wasn't on the agenda because it was Jimmy's birthday! He was the last of the gang to turn eleven (so it was a really big deal!), and his mum and dad had organized a party at his house.

The Lindo family's house was one of the prettiest

in the village. The pastel blue thatched cottage had a stream running alongside it and a little driveway edged with wild flowers, which led to a beautiful rose-covered door. It was a world away from the east London concrete city Jimmy's Jamaican family had lived in before moving to Little Alverton.

Billy, Anna and Andy dumped their bikes near the driveway and walked up to the front door. Just as they were about to ring the bell, the door opened, and an avalanche of smaller kids piled out of the house. Their eyes were lit up in wonder as they chattered among themselves with excitement.

'That was the BEST thing I've ever seen!' said one small boy as he walked past them.

'I know! Those animals are awesome!' his friend replied.

'I can't believe Jimmy put that tarantula on his head!' exclaimed a third boy.

'Or that giant cockroach in his bed, urgh!' said another, and they all giggled.

'Hello, Mrs Lindo,' Billy said, as Jimmy's mum appeared from inside, looking rather bewildered. 'What's going on?'

'Children, I cannot believe what Jimmy is doing to me, on his birthday! His love of nature is getting out of control!'

As they walked inside, Jimmy's exhausted-looking dad came to join them in the hallway, the sound of horse racing echoing from the TV in the front room. 'It's not love, it's an *obsession*,' he said, sighing. 'I told Jimmy that we couldn't afford to keep all the animals he's been bringing home with him. I know he wants to rescue them and of course we want to help, but it's not cheap.'

'Well, it seems Jimmy took that to heart and decided to charge people to come and see the animals,' Mrs Lindo said.

Billy tried to hide a grin and could see that Anna and Andy were doing the same. Typical Jimmy, he'd do anything to keep his animal friends.

And it was true. Jimmy took the TV adverts saying that pets were for life, not just for Christmas, very seriously, and had started taking in animals that would otherwise have found themselves homeless, hoping to eventually find them 'forever homes'. Word had got around and things had slightly spiralled out of control . . . Of course, Jimmy didn't mind as it meant he was surrounded by all kinds of furry and not-so-furry friends. It was just a shame that the food for the animals and the electricity needed to power all the heaters and pumps was very much *not* free.

'But never mind all that,' Mrs Lindo said. 'Why don't you go on up to see Jimmy, while I set things up for the party?'

'Sounds great, Mrs Lindo,' said Billy, running up the stairs with Andy and Anna close behind.

Jimmy's room was something to behold. Jimmy had somehow persuaded his parents to let him set up floor-to-ceiling tanks, each full of life. There were fish of every colour you could imagine, amazing snakes and lizards, not to mention the spiders, scorpions and bugs! The room was alive with colour and movement.

But that wasn't all. Jimmy had even built a makeshift aviary in his back garden and – with the help of Billy and his incredible mind for inventions – fixed a slide to the outside of his bedroom window so he could simply zip down to see his feathered friends whenever he liked. There were canaries, budgies, cockatoos, parakeets . . . all being looked after by Jimmy until they could be set free or find a new family. Since moving to the village, Jimmy had become really good friends with a neighbouring farmer, Mr Miller, who had been teaching him how to look after the animals in the right way, making sure they were all happy and healthy.

It was no wonder that the kids who'd just left had been so impressed with Jimmy's animals: every time the friends went round to his house there seemed to

be a new addition!

'HAPPY BIRTHDAY, JIMMY!' Andy, Billy and Anna cheered as they bounded into his bedroom.

Jimmy was sitting at his desk, carrying out an autopsy on what looked like a mole. He glanced up at them with an unhappy expression on his face.

'Oh my God, Jimmy, that's disgusting,' Anna said. 'What on earth are you doing?!'

Jimmy replied solemnly, 'It's really sad. I found this little fella down by the playing fields. It's only a young mole, and it made me think of the fish and fox we found before discovering that horrible polluting farm. So I wanted to find out what happened. And now I think I have . . .' He held up a plump, pink worm between his gloved fingers. 'This was in his stomach, and I think it's poisoned!'

Anna gasped and Billy and Andy looked on, astonished.

'You're doing that, on your birthday?!' Andy asked.

'Well, my birthday is another story,' said Jimmy, looking uncomfortable. 'I don't want to be ungrateful or anything, but . . . I didn't get what I wanted from Mum and Dad. I was very specific about that Komodo dragon; it's a real gap in the offerings at Jimmy's Zoo!'

Billy laughed and shook his head. 'Jimmy, Komodo dragons are HUGE! There's no way your parents would have got you one of those!'

'I know,' Jimmy sighed. 'But I really did want one.'

'Well, what did you get?' Anna asked, putting a comforting arm around her friend.

Jimmy nodded to the window, and they all rushed over to take a look. In the back garden was a sparkling Raleigh Grifter bike, with bear-trap pedals, mushroom grips for comfort, and stunt pegs on the front and back.

'That's amazing! You lucky thing. That's a beauty of a bike,' Billy said.

'Yeah, I know – I do love it, really. It's just that I had my heart set on the dragon.'

'Well, you might want this, then,' said Billy, handing over a present. Jimmy ripped open the wrapping to reveal a model of a Komodo dragon.

Jimmy grinned. 'Oh, mate, this is amazing! Thank you!'

Anna gave hers next. 'Well, I can challenge that – you might like my one.'

Jimmy ripped the gift open to reveal a T-shirt with a Komodo dragon on it, its tail wrapping around the shoulders. Jimmy put it on immediately, giving Anna a grateful hug.

Then Andy stepped in with his. 'Go on, open it!' he said excitedly.

Jimmy ripped open the present and out burst a load of colourful fluffy wool.

'My auntie knitted you a Komodo dragon tank top,' he said bashfully. It was the most outrageous tank top ever, but it did have a majestic Komodo dragon on the back – although, because Auntie Doreen had used up all the odds and ends in her knitting basket to make it, it looked more like Donald Duck than a killer dragon. Luckily for Andy, Jimmy's eyes lit up.

'This is possibly the best present I've ever had, thank you,' he said, beaming, immediately pulling it on over Anna's T-shirt. Andy sighed with relief.

'Anyway, what are you doing with that mole?' Anna asked.

'Now I've performed the autopsy, I'm going to preserve this small burrowing mammal, just like this one –' Jimmy picked up something from his desk that looked like a rat, then turned it over and unzipped its tummy to reveal a stash of pencils, pens and rubbers, plus a selection of penny sweets. 'See? It's a pencil case! Complete with a sharpener . . .' His friends looked confused for a second, then Jimmy pulled up the tail '. . . for its bum!'

'Jimmy! That's gross!' exclaimed Anna.

'No, that's genius!' said Andy, clearly impressed.

'I guess, at least no one's going to steal your pencils!' Billy said, looking revolted.

Jimmy loved his party. His mum and dad had created an animal-themed treasure hunt, with clues all around the house and garden for them to solve. For every question they got right they were awarded a handful of sweets, from sherbet Dip Dabs to Flying Saucers, Black Jacks, Fruit Salads and everything in between.

Then it was time for the bumps – the birthday ritual that every child had to go through. (Was it pleasure or punishment? It depended on how kind your friends were . . .) Everyone took a leg and an arm and bumped Jimmy up and down in the air – one for each of his eleven years on planet earth, plus one for luck.

Wherever you looked, the animal theme was strong. There was even an animal-inspired buffet. Mr and Mrs Lindo had upgraded the regular pigs in blankets by instead wrapping bacon round Jimmy's favourite food, fish fingers, and had linked a load of them together in the shape of a giant rattlesnake. The contrast of smoky bacon, crunchy breadcrumb coating and flaky fish with the ketchup head and mayonnaise rattle tail was surprisingly next-level delicious. *Definitely one to suggest at home*, Billy thought. There was a ham, pineapple and Cheddar cheese hedgehog, his mum's extra-special jerk chicken that had been pulled off the bone, then put into animal moulds with rice and popped out into animal shapes, and a watermelon rabbit. Not to mention a frog made out of grapes, and King Louie from *The Jungle Book*, created using sliced ham for the body and segments of orange for his face.

But, of course, what all the kids were waiting for was the cake. Mrs Lindo's Jamaican ginger cake was legendary! And for Jimmy's birthday she'd taken a cake, cut it up and stacked it into a pyramid, then his dad had used his brilliant plastering talents to smother the whole thing in different flavours of ice cream (he had to work fast to avoid it melting!), before pebble-dashing it with hundreds and thousands and finishing it with sparklers. It was one spectacular birthday cake! Everyone sang 'Happy Birthday to You' in front of the cake and Billy took a Polaroid picture of the wonderful scene.

'Mum, you know what would make my birthday?' Jimmy said.

'What's that, my precious?' she replied.

'Billy, Anna and Andy staying over. Pleeeeeeease?'

'Well, I suppose it is your birthday . . . OK, let me call their parents and make sure they're happy for them to stay.'

Before she could say anything else, the kids rushed back up to Jimmy's room and settled in for the night, although Andy had to admit he was slightly nervous about sleeping in a room full of snakes that potentially could escape!

They spent the rest of the evening talking about their summer plans.

'I can't wait to get back to Balthazar to see Basil

and the other Sprites,' Billy said. 'There's so much exploring still to do!'

'Yep, this summer is going to be epic,' Jimmy agreed. 'And this birthday has been my best ever, too.'

Eventually their chatter quietened down as the four friends fell asleep, dreaming of all the adventures that Waterfall Woods might hold for them over the next few weeks.

Early the next morning, Billy was woken up by a burning feeling on his chest.

'Ow!' he yelped.

'What is it?' Anna said, rubbing her eyes and throwing pillows at Jimmy and Andy to wake them up.

'It's my flint necklace! It's glowing and burning – just like it did before when the Boonas were about to attack,' Billy said. He looked down at the special necklace he'd been given by Chief Mirren as a way of keeping in touch with the Sprites. It was only supposed to be used in an emergency. What was going on?

Letters started to appear on the necklace:

COME QUICK! WE NEED YOUR HELP! UNDER ATTACK.

Billy looked at his friends in shock and confusion.

'Maybe there's a problem with the Rhythm again,' Anna said worriedly.

'"Under attack" sounds more dramatic,' Jimmy said. 'It sounds like the Sprites are in real trouble.'

'Well, our friends need help, whatever it is, so we'd better go and find out what's going on,' said Billy.

Chapter 2

Where's Wilfred?

Quick as a flash, the kids got dressed and ran out of the house. Jimmy's parents weren't up yet, so he left a note for them to say that they'd decided to head to holiday club early.

'I'd better go and get my backpack,' Billy said, thinking of the bag full of essential gadgets for sticky situations that he stashed back in his treehouse. 'It might come in handy! I'll be quick, and I'll meet you at the woods.'

'Roger that, Beefburger One,' Jimmy said, using Billy's walkie-talkie nickname.

'That gives me an idea!' Anna said. 'Jimmy, grab your walkie-talkie from inside, and Billy, you get yours when you head home. That way we can keep in touch until we're back together again.'

'Good thinking!' Billy said with a grin. 'I'll be back as soon as I can!' He spun his bike in the dirt and headed off at top speed back through the village towards home, the Green Giant pub.

Billy made the journey in record time. The thought of Basil and the Sprites being in danger had his feet moving like lightning! It was still early, but his dad was already up, getting the pub ready for opening.

'Hey, Dad! Sorry, can't stop – on my way to that holiday club,' Billy said.

'Good on ya, son,' his dad replied. 'You know what I always say: If you're early, you're on time; if you're on time, you're late; and if you're late, that's unacceptable – you're toast!'

'I know, Dad,' said Billy, who'd heard it a million times before. 'Love you!' And he ran to the treehouse.

He quickly clambered up the ladder. There, hanging on a mannequin, was the backpack. It was full to the brim with all kinds of tools and inventions that might help out at any given moment – Billy had been adding to it for the last few weeks, so it was full to bursting now. He snatched the bag and picked up his walkie-talkie from the floor.

'This is Beefburger One. Over!' Billy said. **'I have the bag and I'm on my way. Over.'**
Tsccchhhhh!

'Beefburger One, this is Thunderbug!' Jimmy's voice echoed in the treehouse. **'We have a problem. Repeat, we have a problem. Police and police dogs everywhere! Over.'**

Tsccchhhhh!

'This is Sassy Cat.' Anna's voice came through the walkie-talkie. **'They're talking about Wilfred being reported missing! The police aren't letting anyone near the woods. Over.'**

Billy's heart sank. This was a disaster.

Tsccchhhhh!

'Pie here!' Andy's voice piped up. **'I've got a plan, leave it to me. I just need you to grab me a few things from the pub kitchen, Billy!'** There was a short silence and then: **'Oops, I mean Beefburger One, and uh . . . Over!'**

'Sure thing, Pie,' Billy replied. **'Anything you need. Over.'**

Ten minutes later, Billy was back with his friends just a few metres away from the elm tree that catapulted them over the wall surrounding the woods. There were several police officers and dogs standing by the tree, blocking their only way in.

On his way from the pub, Billy had ridden past

Wilfred's house and seen police cars parked in the drive. There was lots of activity as people in uniform buzzed around looking important. Wilfred Revel had always been a loner, so they'd assumed no one would notice the fact he'd been away for a few weeks, but it seemed someone had, and now the police were clearly trying to work out where the old man was.

Billy thought about the mess they'd left in the house the night they'd taken Wilfred to the woods to meet his brother. Andy had smashed his piggy bank and they'd left behind some of the pie Wilfred had cooked, so that would still be there getting mouldy. Billy was pretty sure they hadn't even closed the back door. It wasn't surprising that it looked suspicious!

'Here's what you asked for, Andy,' Billy said, handing his friend a bag of goodies from the pub.

Andy peered inside. 'Sausages, bacon, bread, cheese, crisps, mustard, pickles, tinfoil . . . Perfect!'

'So what's the plan?' Jimmy asked, intrigued. 'You wouldn't tell us anything until Billy got here.'

'Just leave it to me,' said Andy. 'I know what I'm doing. I'll give you as long as I can, so you can get

29

into the woods – I'll meet you there later. Jimmy, give me your walkie-talkie, then I can radio if I need to.'

With that, Andy got to work with speed and precision, taking the bacon and sausages and piling them into the rolls, along with the pickles and cheese, all finished with a flourish of mustard. He paid particular attention to one roll, which he added extra toppings to. Then he made one filled with cheese and crushed crisps. Finally, he wrapped them up in tinfoil, stuffing the two 'special' ones in the waistband of his trousers.

'What are those for?' asked Billy.

'Don't worry about those,' Andy said, with a glint in his eye. 'You three sneak down as far as you can towards the entrance to the woods and leave me to deal with the

30

dogs. I've got a little trick my uncle taught me to keep them off your scent – now, go!'

Billy, Anna and Jimmy made for the edge of Waterfall Woods, watching on in wonder as Andy, Master of Mayhem, conducted the most wonderfully chaotic scene.

With absolute confidence, Andy tied several of the sausage sarnies on to the back of his bike with string, almost like you would with tin cans on a wedding car. He then cycled as fast as he could past the police standing at the edge of the woods, catching everyone's attention with the weirdness of the scene. The dogs started barking and pulling on their leads to follow him, with the police officers struggling to control them.

Andy swerved round and raced past them again, this time pulling out a roll from his waistband and, riding no-handed, tearing it into bite-size chunks. As he cycled away, he threw little bits of the loaded sausage roll behind him. As professional and well trained as the police dogs were, no one, it seemed, could ever come between a dog and a sausage. Andy

kept going, following an erratic path through the village, while the dogs followed the irresistible scent of sausage, and mayhem ensued!

With the police now distracted, and Little Alverton in chaos, Andy activated the second part of his plan. He knew that nothing travelled faster through a village than hot gossip, so, as he raced up towards Wilfred's house, he stopped and breathlessly told a group of locals that he'd seen Wilfred at the bowls club. And he was right – the news travelled faster than he could cycle – and, by the time he reached the entrance to the alleyway that led to the bowls club, a swarm of police and people were already there.

'HE'S OVER THERE!' he shouted. Everyone started piling through the alleyway, leaving the coast clear for

his friends to use the elm tree to spring themselves
over the wall and into the woods.

Tsccchhhhh!

'You're good to go, guys, from Pie,' Andy
announced proudly on his walkie-talkie.

Tsccchhhhh!

Anna whooped and said, **'That was amazing.
Over!'**

Tsccchhhhh!

'How did you do that? Over!' said Billy in
complete awe.

Tsccchhhhh!

**'Andy, you've gone from liability to legend!
There's only one Andy. Over,'** said Jimmy.

Tsccchhhhh!

'Ahhh, I'll take that, thank me later, guys,' said Andy.

With no time to wait for Andy to say 'Over!', Billy, Anna and Jimmy flew over the wall and raced into the dappled wood, the summer sun breaking through the leaves. Soon they were in front of a familiar old friend, the gnarly oak tree – the gate to the magical world of Waterfall Woods. Billy was always struck with wonder whenever he saw the tree; he couldn't believe they had accidentally discovered a portal to another world just by randomly hugging it!

He took a running jump and leapt at the tree, wrapping his legs and arms round it in a giant hug. Billy felt the familiar vibration ripple through his body, only for it to disappear a moment later. He wasn't sure if he'd ever get used to the feeling, no matter how many times they opened the gate.

The others followed, and, just like that, they moved from their world of chaos to the tranquillity and vibrancy of the magical one. Immediately the air felt cleaner and fresher, things were greener and more alive. And, as they hugged the tree to close the gate

behind them, there was a beautiful, unique hum of birds, bugs and wildlife in the air. They all took a moment to take in the scene.

'The Rhythm feels fine – you can hear the animals are OK,' said Jimmy. The kids nodded in agreement.

'Yeah, everything seems fine here,' Billy said, looking around. 'Ow!' He looked down at his necklace as the familiar burning pain hit him, and another message appeared:

PLEASE COME QUICKLY!
WE'RE AT BALTHAZAR.
HIDING FROM THE RED
WOMAN.

'The red woman?' Anna said. 'Who's that?'

'There's only one way to find out. Let's get going,' Billy said.

'Let's find the buzzpacks and get there as quickly as we can,' Jimmy agreed.

They all looked at each other with determined faces and Billy knew nothing was going to stop them from saving their friends. Before they'd all witnessed the power of the magic woods, Billy and the gang would probably have been filled with self-doubt about what lay in store and whether they could handle it.

But now they all knew the importance of the woods and that the balance of the Rhythm was bigger than they were. These woods had taught them so many things already, including the need to protect the ones you love, no matter what. So here they were, bravely running towards danger without excuses or second thoughts. Either that, or they were naively running into a whole load of trouble . . .

Chapter 3

The Battle for Balthazar

The amazing thing about going through the oak-tree gate into the magical world was how MASSIVE the woods suddenly became. Billy still couldn't quite believe how different the woods were once they'd left their village behind. Luckily, the buzzpacks they'd found in the cabin near Bilfred's garden meant they could soar across the woods at speed! They'd even stashed a few extras near this secret entrance just in case any of them stopped working. As Billy always said, you could never be too prepared!

Billy loved using the buzzpacks, but every time they did, deep inside he also worried that their true owner would soon notice they'd gone and wouldn't be happy about it – he certainly wouldn't be happy if anyone borrowed his gadgets without asking. What if it was even the reason Balthazar was being attacked? Could it be his fault that his friends were in trouble? It wouldn't be the first time . . .

He tried to push down his doubt and worry as he swivelled his backpack around to the front, so he could pull on the buzzpack. There was no time for that now. He had to stay focused! If this was his fault, then it was even more important that he helped to fix it.

The kids rose into the air together and shot as fast as they could towards their Sprite friends. They skimmed the tips of the trees, followed rivers through the valleys and up, up the mountain, before diving down into the incredible, breathtaking area that surrounded Balthazar.

As soon as the Sprite city came into view, with Balthazar Castle standing proudly on the side of the volcano, it was clear that things were not OK. Usually, Balthazar was serene and peaceful, but in front of them was a new kind of chaos. Billy signalled for Anna and Jimmy to follow him and they hovered behind a rock face, staying out of sight so they could scope out what was happening.

They looked on as dozens of silhouettes in buzzpacks just like theirs flew around the castle, firing what seemed to be some kind of weapon. The figures were not much bigger than the

kids, and even though they looked human in shape and size, their movements were too jerky and fast to be human – in fact, they looked totally out of place within the natural world around them.

'What are those things?' Jimmy whispered, hovering closer to Billy.

'I don't know, but I really don't like the look of them,' Billy replied. 'I think they might be . . . robots?'

'And those weapons they have are pretty weird, too,' Anna whispered. 'Look, it's like a sound wave or something coming out of them.'

Anna was right. As the figures blasted their weapons, they didn't fire bullets or bombs, but instead ominous blurry ripples that seemed to wipe out anything living or growing in their path, leaving bare earth behind.

Billy thought back to when they'd first discovered Balthazar with Basil all those weeks ago. After years of being abandoned, Balthazar had been run-down and unloved but, in no time at all, the Sprites had transformed it back to its former glory, thanks to their incredible ability to work as a team. Now, it was being destroyed swiftly by whatever these flying creatures were. Every ripply wave had the power to strip a tree of its leaves and send wildlife hurtling for cover.

'What are they doing?' Anna said, fury in her voice. 'They are destroying Balthazar!'

'I suppose we know who owns these buzzpacks now,' Jimmy said, wide-eyed. 'And they're definitely not friendly.'

'Where are Bilfred, Wilfred and the Sprites?' Billy said with worry in his voice.

They all looked at each other with fear. No wonder their friends had needed their help so desperately!

Billy pulled out his necklace. 'Where are you, Basil?' he said, clutching the flint.

A moment later a reply etched into the stone:

HIDING UNDERGROUND, IN THE MOUNTAIN, THROUGH THE GREEN WATERFALL! QUICK!

Billy immediately felt a rush of relief.

'Green waterfall?' Anna said, peering at the message. 'I don't remember seeing one of those.'

They all scanned the valley, Billy pulling the hood

of his modified backpack over his head to use the binoculars.

'Look! Each waterfall does have a slightly different colour!' he said to the others. 'They go along in the order of the rainbow.' He pointed to a waterfall just behind the ransacked city. 'There's the green one!'

'Good spot, Billy,' said Anna. 'Right, now we just need to get there without being seen. How are we going to do that?'

'Let's fly as close as we can under the cover of the woods, then hide our buzzpacks and go on foot. We don't want these things, whatever they are, spotting us,' Billy said.

They started whirling and winding, ducking and diving their way through the trees, making sure they didn't get thwacked by branches or taken out by rocks. In normal circumstances this would've been a lot of fun, but there was no time to waste. As they got deeper into the valley, the undergrowth became thicker and denser, greener and more lush, making it too tight to fly any more. So they glided down to the ground.

'How on earth are we going to get through that?'

Anna asked, unable to see a way beyond the greenery.

Billy pulled two drawstrings on his backpack, and revealed a compartment with an array of screwdrivers, pliers, scissors, nail clippers and mini hammers, all in numbered order, with the last being a set of razor-sharp shears. 'Who would like to do some pruning?' he said with a smile.

'Nice one, Billy!' Anna said, grabbing the shears and immediately trying to open them – but they seemed to be stuck.

Billy reached out and took them, saying, 'Here, let me. There's a bit of a knack to it –'

Anna snatched them back. 'I can do it!' She released a catch, freeing the blades, and started hacking her way through the undergrowth like a hot knife through butter.

Billy looked at Jimmy in confusion. He had started to notice that, recently, every time he offered any kind of help to Anna, she seemed to reject it. He didn't understand why. Anna was always the first one to help him out, but when he tried to do the same, she just got cross. Billy was baffled – who didn't like help? It was the best thing in the world.

Jimmy shrugged and Billy switched his thoughts back to the job at hand, noticing Anna had hacked a clear path all the way through to the edge of the forest. The boys followed her along it.

Without looking at Billy, Anna passed him the shears to slip into his backpack. Billy tried to ignore the obvious cold shoulder, but he couldn't help feeling annoyed that she was getting cross about something so silly.

Suddenly, a buzzing sound filled the air, and all thoughts of their argument were instantly forgotten. The friends hid in the tree roots as a troop of four large flying figures landed just metres in front of them.

They were now close enough to get a better look. The gizmo geek in Billy couldn't help but notice that the robots' buzzpacks were slightly different to theirs –

more streamlined and shinier, with extra buttons. They did have the same blue stone in the middle, which the kids had worked out powered the packs, but even that was bigger; Billy assumed it gave them more power or something.

'Wh . . . Wh . . . Who is that?' Jimmy stuttered, pointing to an ominous figure in a red dress in the distance. The lady was carrying a staff which had a glowing blue stone at the top. A huge dog stood by her side, its slick coat glinting a weird grey-green in the sun and its piercing yellow eyes scanning the horizon for movement.

The woman reached down to pat the dog on the head. And then another dog appeared, tilting its head up to be scratched behind the ears . . . Billy gasped. It wasn't another dog – the dog had TWO heads! One was slightly smaller than the other, but four eyes gazed up at the woman in total admiration, two sets of fangs open and dripping with slobber.

Billy whispered, 'Whoa, do you see that? That's no ordinary dog!'

'I've never seen anything like it,' Jimmy said,

his mouth open. 'It's amazing.'

'Um . . . not so amazing if it smells us, Jimmy!' Anna said. 'I don't reckon even Andy's sausage sandwiches could save us from THAT!'

'Don't worry, they won't smell us, we're downwind,' Jimmy replied, sounding pretty confident. 'I think we're OK – for now!'

'Wait,' Billy said, remembering something. 'Didn't Wilfred and Bilfred both mention a two-headed dog being with the woman who took Bilfred? Remember? Could that be the same lady?'

Anna and Jimmy gasped. Was Billy right? Was that why she was here? To get Bilfred back?

The lady stood elegantly on a piece of rock that jutted out from the drawbridge at the entrance to the city. She gracefully moved her arms, as if conducting an orchestra, but instead of music she was creating wave after wave of attacks from the battalions of buzzpacks. All with just a flick of her hand or a point of her staff.

'Whoever she is, she's definitely in charge,' Jimmy said.

'And she's trying to attack our friends!' Billy added.

'She's awful, but . . .' Anna started, her eyes fixed on the woman.

'But what?' asked Jimmy.

'She's more frightening than anything I've ever seen – I mean, look at her: tall, calm and totally in control – but she's also so beautifully powerful,' said Anna in wonder. 'And doesn't she look too young to have been around when Wilfred and Bilfred were just kids?'

'Well, yeah, she doesn't look like your typical evil witch – no wrinkles, crooked nose, or warty face,' Billy said.

'That's just from books; this is real life,' Jimmy said. 'You can be beautiful and utterly scary, like, really scary.'

'You're right, Jimmy! Let's call her Scary Red,' said Anna.

Suddenly, their view was blocked as more buzzpack-wearing things landed near them. The three friends crouched right down, scared of being seen.

'You know what, I think you're right, Billy,' Jimmy

said quietly. 'They're not human. Look at their shoulders and legs.'

Billy wriggled around to get a better view, looking through the binoculars on the hood of his backpack. They had human-looking heads, hands and feet, but their arms, legs and shoulders shimmered with silver, and they were covered in metal muscles and tendons, made of bionic machinery.

'204, did you set the traps around the front of the drawbridge?' one droid asked – it sounded almost human, but monotone, without any kind of personality, and

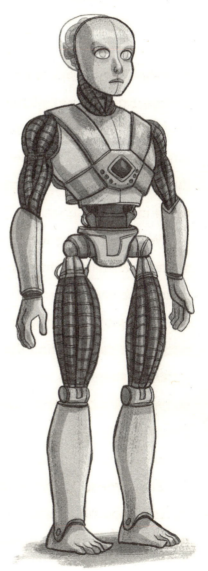

the 'voice' echoed straight out of its head rather than through the 'mouth' that was etched on to its face.

'Yes, 205,' another droid replied.

'Our leader has instructed that we are not to use firepower, only sonic booms. There's potential danger underneath the castle,' 205 said.

Scary Red raised her hands in the air. 'Grower 162, Bilfred Revel,' she announced. Her voice echoed through the air, somehow amplified by each and every robot circling Balthazar – it was as if she was everywhere, making for an epic, and incredibly spooky, sound. 'You must return to your garden where you belong, or my Rangers will spend every minute of every hour of every day destroying this city and its occupants until we find you.'

When there was no reply, a flick of her wrist summoned a deluge of sonic booms from every direction. 'You are mine; you work for me. We are all at the service of Terra Nova. You WILL fulfil your purpose.'

'That proves it,' Billy said with a gulp, fear rising in his stomach. 'She must be the one who trapped Bilfred in that garden and takes all his fruit and veg.'

'But what does she mean, "at the service of Terra Nova"?' Anna asked.

The others shrugged in confusion. There were so many mysteries in these woods that it was hard to keep up.

Billy waved Anna and Jimmy closer, so their heads touched. 'This is way bigger than I first thought, guys. I'm really scared. Scary Red trapped Bilfred for years! I'm . . . I'm not sure I can handle this. It's another level from battling Boonas with Scotch eggs!'

'We're all scared, Billy. But what do you suggest we do – go home and tell our parents?' Anna said. 'We can't do that. We're here now and we can do something. Don't you want to help our friends?'

'Of course I do! But really? Against robot Rangers, Scary Red, two-headed dogs with fangs? This is stuff that armies would struggle to deal with, let alone three kids, a gizmo backpack and some garden shears!'

'Very sharp garden shears, though, Billy,' Jimmy said with a wink.

'Well, I think we should talk to Basil on the flint

and find out exactly where everyone is. I'm sure we can get them out – escape routes are our speciality!' said Anna, with a determined glint in her eye.

'But this is seriously dangerous. And . . . I can't always protect you!' Billy said. As if on cue, a sonic boom shook the ground not far away from them.

There was an uncomfortable silence. 'I don't need you to look after me,' Anna said. 'I can look after myself. And I'm not going home. Are you, Jimmy?'

'No, and neither are you, Billy,' he said, patting his best friend on the shoulder. 'We're a team, right?'

'I was really worried you were going to say that!' Billy said, a smile twitching at the corners of his mouth. 'OK, so what do we do?'

'I told you my plan,' said Anna, annoyed that no one had acknowledged her idea.

'I know, but I don't think they'll be able to tell us any more on the flint,' said Billy, finding his confidence again. 'I say we keep moving towards the waterfall.'

Anna crossed her arms in annoyance. 'What do you think, Jimmy?'

Jimmy looked between his two friends, unsure.

'Maybe we should check in on Andy before we do anything?' he suggested.

'Let's try him now on the walkie-talkie . . .' Billy said with a nod.

Tsccchhhhh!

'Any breakers, any takers, Beefburger One here, looking for Pie? Over.'

The three waited for a reply.

Suddenly a crackle came over the line.

Tsccchhhhh!

'I'm at the tree . . . Coming through . . .'

Tsccchhhhh!

Then nothing but the noise of static.

'The valley must be stopping the signal getting here,' said Billy. 'But at least we know he's OK and on his way.'

'Come on. If we're going, let's go,' said Anna. 'There's a ledge up there in the waterfall. I bet it will lead us to a way inside.' And she started marching towards the rock face.

'Wait,' said Billy, gazing up at the slippery rocks. 'It looks tricky. We should take it slow and steady.'

'There's no time for being careful,' Anna said. 'We have to get to our friends. Come on, I'm the best climber between us, I'll lead the way.'

'Maybe Billy is right–' Jimmy began, but quickly stopped when Anna glared at him. 'I mean . . . we're right behind you!'

Jimmy gave Billy a pat on the back and strode after Anna. Billy stayed where he was, watching as Anna started climbing with confident movements. His worry began to fade. After all, she was the best climber, maybe he shouldn't have been so protective. She made it look easy . . .

'Argh!' Anna cried. Her foot had lost its grip on a slippery stone, and she slid down to the bottom.

'Anna!' Billy rushed forward. 'Are you OK?'

Anna huffed. 'I'm fine! Stop fussing, Billy. It was just more slippery than I realized.'

'I told you to be careful!' Billy said. 'Why didn't you listen? You could have really hurt yourself.'

'I didn't though. It was only a small slip. Stop worrying. Come on, we haven't got time for this.'

Anna dusted herself off and started up the rocks again. Billy was sure she had hurt herself and just didn't want to admit it. Billy couldn't understand why she was so annoyed at him when he was only trying to be a good friend.

But as Jimmy disappeared after her into the mist of the waterfall, Billy realized Anna was right about one thing: they really didn't have time for petty arguments. With a sigh, he followed his friends up the cliff, carefully placing his feet so he didn't slip as Anna had done.

Eventually he made it to the top ledge where Anna and Jimmy were waiting.

'Wow!' said Jimmy, holding his hands over his ears as the water slapped down on the rocks. 'This is pretty epic!'

Clearly not wanting to hang around, Anna walked on, straight through the torrent of water, gasping as the incredibly clear, incredibly cold water pounded down on her head. Jimmy followed closely. But Billy, ever prepared, activated the pop-up rainbow umbrella he had in the top of his backpack. It wasn't quite up to surviving the weight of the water pouring down, but at least he wasn't totally soaked to the bone!

Behind the waterfall, they found themselves in a stunning polished-stone cavern, hollowed out by millions of years of water, the walls stripy with wave after wave of different-coloured rocks.

'Where now?' asked Jimmy. 'It doesn't look like there's anything here.'

'Hmm, there must be more to this,' replied Billy. 'Keep searching.'

'Hey, look!' said Anna, pointing excitedly to a small dot at the very base of the cave. It was a little mother-of-pearl seashell, glistening in the streams of light that shot through gaps in the water.

'That's just like the one at the entrance to Balthazar!' Jimmy said. 'It's a Sprite door key!'

Anna nodded and placed her little finger in the middle of the shell. She gently pushed and twisted it, moving it slightly back into the rock. There was a rumble, and then, sure enough, a small entrance leading to a secret tunnel opened up. A smile returned to her face.

'Well done, Anna,' Billy said. She smiled at him and Billy hoped that meant they could put the argument behind them. Then the three friends hurried through and into the volcano.

As soon as they were through the door, the rock closed behind them, leaving the kids in a pitch-black tunnel with the sound of dripping water in the distance.

'Please tell me you've got some lights in that backpack of yours, Billy,' Jimmy said.

'No problemo, my friend!' Billy replied, and after scrambling around in his bag he handed both of his friends a torch.

'What about you?' Jimmy asked, turning on his torch, its beam lighting up the tunnel around them.

Billy grinned. 'One, two, three, let there be light!'

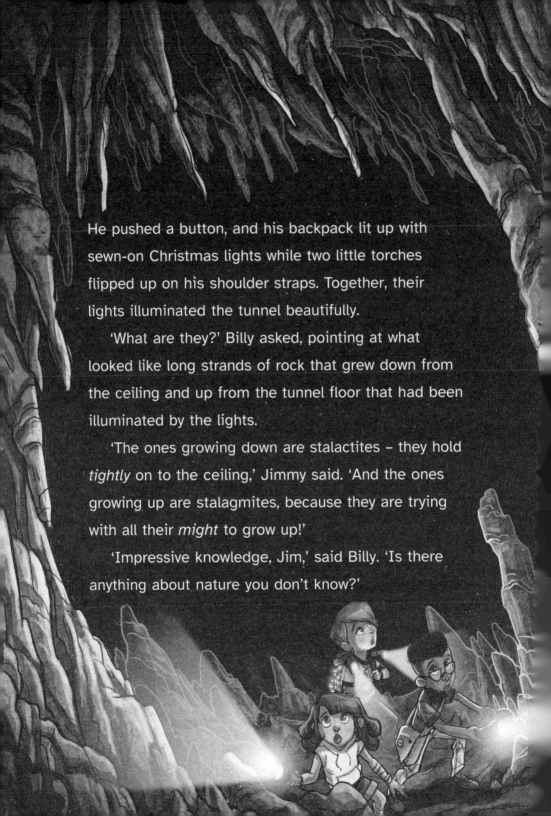

He pushed a button, and his backpack lit up with sewn-on Christmas lights while two little torches flipped up on his shoulder straps. Together, their lights illuminated the tunnel beautifully.

'What are they?' Billy asked, pointing at what looked like long strands of rock that grew down from the ceiling and up from the tunnel floor that had been illuminated by the lights.

'The ones growing down are stalactites – they hold *tightly* on to the ceiling,' Jimmy said. 'And the ones growing up are stalagmites, because they are trying with all their *might* to grow up!'

'Impressive knowledge, Jim,' said Billy. 'Is there anything about nature you don't know?'

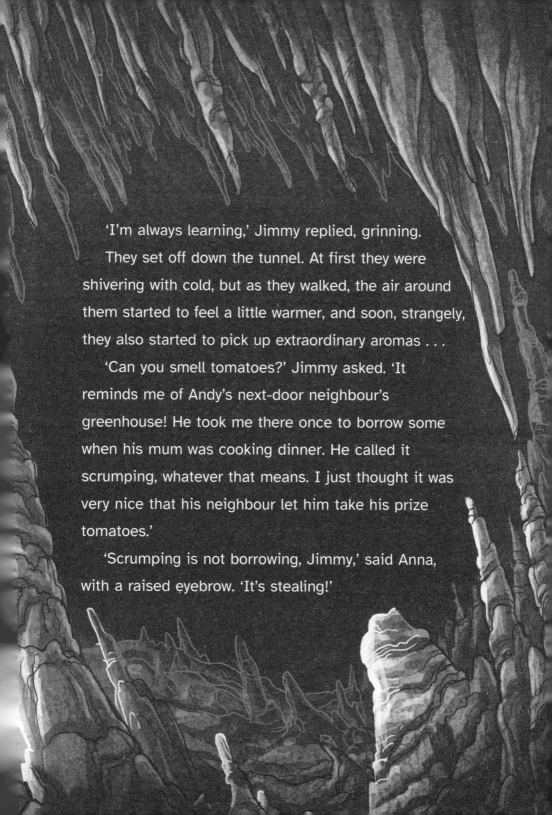

'I'm always learning,' Jimmy replied, grinning.

They set off down the tunnel. At first they were shivering with cold, but as they walked, the air around them started to feel a little warmer, and soon, strangely, they also started to pick up extraordinary aromas . . .

'Can you smell tomatoes?' Jimmy asked. 'It reminds me of Andy's next-door neighbour's greenhouse! He took me there once to borrow some when his mum was cooking dinner. He called it scrumping, whatever that means. I just thought it was very nice that his neighbour let him take his prize tomatoes.'

'Scrumping is not borrowing, Jimmy,' said Anna, with a raised eyebrow. 'It's stealing!'

The smell got stronger and stronger until suddenly Billy could make out a twinkle of light in the distance. It wasn't long before the tunnel widened, and they realized the twinkle was a fire with a very large cooking pot nestled on top.

Billy's heart leapt as he saw the giant figure of Bilfred walking towards the pot, crouching down so as not to hit his head on the low ceiling of the tunnel.

'Bilfred!' Billy cried, running towards his friend, with Anna and Jimmy hot on his heels.

At the sight of the kids, the whole cave erupted in excited cheering and clapping as flurries of Sprites flew down from hiding places around the cave. Wilfred appeared too, smiling broadly.

'Oh, Bilfred, Wilfred, aren't you guys a sight for sore eyes!' Billy said, as they reunited.

Bilfred chuckled, scooping Billy up into the tightest hug, lifting him off the ground. 'We feel exactly the same – hello, my dear friends!' he said, tears welling up in his eyes.

'Is that a little tear I see, Bilfred?' Anna teased, her smile beaming from ear to ear as

she stood on tiptoes and used her sleeve to gently wipe it away.

'Could well be, young Anna,' he replied. 'I'm so glad you've come to help us.'

It might have been the fire, it might have been the welcome, but even though danger lurked outside, all everyone could feel was the most incredible warmth from the tops of their heads to the tips of their toes. But it wasn't to last . . .

Chapter 4

The Capture

Once the cheering and hugging had quietened down, Billy was surprised by how calm the caves felt – it was the total opposite of the chaos happening outside. There were small candles dotted around nooks and crannies in the curved wall where Sprites had nestled themselves for safety, making the cave look like a mini amphitheatre.

The only thing that reminded them of the danger just above the surface was the sonic booms that seemed to come in erratic waves, causing some of the Sprites to dash for cover as stalactites dropped and shattered from the ceiling of the cave.

Billy, Jimmy and Anna huddled around the fire as Bilfred and Wilfred took it in turns to stir the giant cooking pot.

'That smells amazing,' Jimmy said. 'What is it?'

'This is what we call garden soup – well, I guess it's cave soup now – made from lots of lovely veg. You see, when Balthazar was attacked, Chief Mirren told us to take cover, hide in these caves and feed the troops,' explained Bilfred. 'And that's when me and Wilfred had a brainwave.'

'We took inspiration from our dad and grabbed as much veg as we could, plus some secret herbs and spices, because he was a cook in the army . . .' Wilfred carried on.

'. . . And he always said, "Keep cooking and carry on, make soup, not war," do you remember, Wilfred? There was nothing he couldn't cook – his roasts were legendary!'

'They were. He always made massive Yorkshire puddings, and his home-grown horseradish blew our heads off! He always reckoned, if the troops aren't fed, you've got no options; if everyone's starving, you have to surrender, and we didn't want that, did we?'

'No, and we all know that soup is the best way to keep spirits high, so we got a big vat of this on the go – and it's a blooming good one, even if I do say so myself!' Bilfred replied with a chuckle.

'And who knows how long we'll be here,' Wilfred added. 'So we said to ourselves that we might as well save our energy for when it's really needed – and you kids should do the same. We're snug as bugs down here, so dry off and let's catch up over some good food.'

Another boom covered everyone in a layer of dust, but it didn't seem to bother Bilfred or Wilfred, who simply brushed the dust off each other and carried on cooking. There was something so special about being brothers that just made them feel safe around one another.

Billy couldn't resist asking about the little ship that was floating on top of the soup, carrying smouldering cinders of twigs. 'What on earth is that in your soup?' he asked.

'Ahhh,' said Bilfred, his eyes twinkling. 'That, my friend, is a smoke float. What I do is I take my little tin boat here and fill it with all kinds of woody herbs and fruit-tree twigs, then I set light to them. Look at the smoke – it wafts up, curls around and comes back down, licking the simmering broth with its smoky herby flavours. It's absolutely scrumdiddlyumptious!' Even in the depths of the tunnel the kids could see Bilfred looking happy with himself.

Bilfred ladled them all out some soup. 'Eat up – you too, little ones,' he said, beckoning his Sprite friends to fill their tiny shell bowls. 'Then we can tell you what's been going on.'

Wilfred nodded. 'Basil will want to see you, too – he's up top with Chief Mirren. He'll be pleased you got the message that we needed help.'

Billy took a slurp from his bowl and exclaimed, 'Oh my, that's one of the nicest soups I've ever tasted. Just what you need when you're shivering with cold!'

And it truly was something special. Sweet, smoky and herby, the soup was full of chunks of succulent veggies, along with beans and multicoloured grains that looked like rice. A slurp here, a nibble there and a bite of dumpling to finish – it was just what the doctor ordered. Within seconds Billy felt a rush of energy surge through his body.

'So tell us what's going on here,' Anna said. 'And what are these tunnels?'

'Turns out the Giants and Sprites built these tunnels together when Balthazar was built,' Bilfred said. 'They were to store things that needed to be kept cool, but were also a network of escape routes for moments just like this.'

'So even when this place was first created, they were preparing for the worst?' Jimmy said. 'Like they always knew something like this could happen.'

'It is awful out there,' said Anna. 'A scary lady in red is orchestrating an attack on Balthazar, and we think she might be the one who trapped you in the garden all those years ago, Bilfred.'

'She's back?' Bilfred's eyes widened. 'You mean she's the one attacking Balthazar? Do you think it's because of me? Because I left the garden?'

'Yeah, we think so,' Jimmy said quietly.

'But what's really weird is that she looks so young. So how can she be the same one who attacked you both over fifty years ago?' Anna said.

'Maybe there are lots of scary red ladies?' suggested Billy, thinking that would be even more terrifying than just one of them.

'Or she's discovered the secret to eternal youth,' scoffed Jimmy.

'Don't be silly, Jimmy,' Anna replied. 'She'd be a

millionaire if that were true.'

'She'll be gone soon though, won't she?' Bilfred asked. 'You know, she'll pass, like a storm.'

'It doesn't seem like they're going anywhere,' said Billy. 'We heard her say she's going to spend every minute of every hour of every day destroying the city until she finds you.'

There was an uncomfortable silence as the truth sank in.

'I think it's time we go and speak to Basil and Chief Mirren,' said Billy.

'Of course,' said Wilfred. 'We need to stay here and look after our Sprite friends. But I'm sure someone will show you the way.'

A few Sprite volunteers flew down to help. They led the kids through a network of tunnels that eventually popped out in the basement of Balthazar Castle. The closer to the surface they went, the louder the bangs and booms from the sonic attacks became.

They made their way up the stairs to a huge ballroom, where Basil and Chief Mirren were hiding behind a barricade of stone blocks and furniture,

along with two other Sprites that Billy recognized as
Cassia and Rosemary. One side of the ballroom had
huge ornate windows – well, they had been ornate, but
were now full of holes where the glass had shattered
from the attack. The windows faced out on to the
valley, giving them a unique view of Scary Red and
her Rangers.

When Basil spotted his friends, his worried face
immediately broke into a huge smile. 'Yous came! I
knews you would!'

'Welcome back, Billy, Anna and Jimmy. Thank you for coming in our hour of need,' Chief Mirren said. Billy noticed that her usual warm and calm tone was gone and instead worry filled her voice.

'We're not quites sure how we're goings to get out of this ones,' Basil said.

'We're here to help,' Billy said.

'Yes, however we can,' Anna added.

'Have you tried to stop her by freezing time?' Jimmy asked. 'Isn't that a big part of your magic?'

'Yes,' Chief Mirren said. 'When she first arrived, we tried to combine all our magic to freeze time so she couldn't move, but it seems she's too powerful. We've never come across her in these woods, so we don't understand who she is or where she came from.'

'She obviously knows about Bilfred,' Billy said. 'We think she's the lady who trapped him in the garden in the first place.'

Chief Mirren nodded. 'We've heard her talk about Bilfred. It seems his escape may have led her to Balthazar. But we need to understand more about what she's doing in our woods and what role she played in Bilfred's imprisonment.'

'We've tagged her with saffron, so we can track where she goes!' Basil said with a grin. 'Not that she knows about it.'

'Ooh, that's clever. How did you get close enough?' asked Anna.

'One very brave Sprite dive-bombed her,' Chief Mirren said with a smile.

'That'll be me!' said Basil proudly and absolutely without a hint of humbleness. 'I flew over to her and she thoughts I was a fly – she tried to swat me! – but I was so fast, she slapped herself round the face. That's when I administered a good dose of saffron.'

'Well done, Basil!' Billy said, beaming at his friend. Basil glowed with pride.

'Chief Mirren, when we were outside, we overheard the robots saying that Scary Red had forbidden them from using weapons on the volcano. Maybe she thinks it's going to erupt, or something?' asked Billy.

'As you know, until recently we thought Balthazar was just a myth –' Chief Mirren began.

'Until I discovered it again!' Basil interrupted.

Chief Mirren nodded. 'The legends surrounding Balthazar spoke of a huge energy source deep within the volcano. A seam of the most powerful rock: anthisalite. It's not created on earth. It can only be created from the colossal energy of a supernova – the explosion of a dying star.'

'That's mega power!' Jimmy said. 'Like, the most immense power in the universe!'

Chief Mirren nodded. 'It's because of that immense power that anthisalite can be charged with an infinite amount of energy,' Chief Mirren explained.

'WOW!' exclaimed Jimmy, his mind blown. 'So it's like an incredible never-ending battery?'

'How did it get here?' Anna asked.

'The legends say it landed here as a meteorite, just as the volcano was erupting, and it was enveloped by lava and buried deep inside. Having spent more time at Balthazar, myself and the other elders now believe it's this energy that nourishes everything in this valley – it's the reason it is so bountiful and lush.'

'Could anthisalite be blue?' Billy said, an idea forming in his mind.

'It certainly could be – I've never seen anthisalite myself,' answered Chief Mirren. 'Why?'

'Our buzzpacks seem to be powered by the small blue stones,' Billy explained. 'We've never had to charge them. They just always work. I noticed the Rangers out there have the same glowing stones, and Scary Red has got one in her staff too. What if she's not just here for Bilfred? What if she knows the volcano has anthisalite within it and wants it for herself?'

'That can never happen,' Chief Mirren said sternly. 'The energy should flow within the lands for all, it mustn't be stolen for the few. In the wrong hands it could be a disaster. It must only ever be used for good, never bad.'

'Scary Red mentioned a place called Terra Nova,' Anna told Chief Mirren. 'Do you know what she was talking about?'

Chief Mirren shook her head. 'I've never heard of such a place. But as we've all discovered, these woods are much larger than we ever thought possible, and our Sprite community has lived hidden in secret for a long time. We haven't explored the woods for generations – until you youngsters arrived.'

A haunting howl came from outside the walls of the castle, the chilling sound echoing all around the valley. It had to be the two-headed hound. The kids and the Sprites looked out to see that the Rangers had all joined up in a single line, hovering in the air around Balthazar.

'Grower 162, Bilfred Revel!' Scary Red shouted, walking into sight. 'My patience has worn thin. Come out now! Or your friend here will suffer the consequences.'

She pulled a smaller figure into view. Billy gasped as he saw that there, in her icy clutches, was Andy, looking scared and annoyed at the same time.

'Get off me! GET OFF ME!' Andy squealed, squirming in her grip.

'Oh no,' said Anna.

'This changes everything,' Basil said, utterly crestfallen.

Chief Mirren nodded. 'Cassia, please could you go and ask Bilfred and Wilfred to come up from the

tunnels. Basil is right: with Andy captured, things have changed.'

As Wilfred looked out of the window, his eyes widened as if he'd seen a ghost. 'It is HER, she's the one who stole my eye and took Bilfred. I'll never forget her face and she hasn't changed one bit!'

'Grower 162. Time's up!' Scary Red roared, clearly becoming impatient. 'Go back to your garden and fulfil your duties now, or this THING, this annoying, irritating, ridiculous brat will be lunch for my darling Death Hound. And we'll start with his delicious squidgy, squodgy eye.'

Andy wailed with fear as the two-headed hound started barking with glee.

Bilfred turned to Wilfred. 'Brother. I can't let Andy get hurt while I cower in here. I have to go back.'

Scary Red's voice boomed again, which ricocheted around Balthazar. 'I never negotiate. You have FIVE seconds . . .'

Bilfred looked at his friends. 'I'm gonna go now.'

'FOUR . . .'

'Is there really no other way?' Billy asked, wiping away a tear.

'THREE . . .'

'No, there isn't,' Bilfred replied. 'We all know that she won't leave without me.' Everyone reluctantly nodded in agreement.

'TWO . . .' Scary Red hovered her mouth over Andy's left eye and started to suck. He squealed in fear as he felt his eye begin to leave its socket.

Bilfred jumped through the broken window out into the open and cried, 'STOP!'

Scary Red stopped and looked up. 'Just in time, Grower 162,' she said. 'Although, I was looking forward to removing this one's eye, as he is disgustingly annoying!' Both heads on the excited dog looked distinctly disappointed, still salivating from the idea of the juicy snack.

Scary Red rose into the air, seemingly powered by her shoes. She sped over to Bilfred and hovered in front of his face, her blue nose ring glinting in the sunlight and red dress billowing in the wind. Billy noticed her shoes glowed blue with the stones in each heel. 'I'm glad you've come to your senses,' she said.

'You have me now. So let Andy go,' Bilfred said.

'Well, I might have lied,' Scary Red said with an evil smile. 'I need to find out who this stray is and how he got here. So I think he'll just have to come with us.'

'I won't talk!' Andy said with as much strength as he could muster.

'I have a feeling that after five days of no food, you might,' Red said with a chilling chuckle.

Andy shook with terror at the thought of a future without three square meals a day plus treats – his mind whirred with the delicious possibilities as he saw Scampi Fries, dry-roasted peanuts, Space Raiders and Flying Saucers disappearing into the distance.

But there was no time for any further protest as Scary Red nodded to her Rangers and in a flash a group had forced Andy's arms behind his back and secured them together using a fine chainmail-like metal that tightened at the touch of a button. At the same time, more Rangers flew up to Bilfred, working together to pull his huge arms behind him to trap him with the chainmail too.

Then, with a sharp look to her Rangers, Scary Red summoned them to pick up her prisoners – Bilfred and Andy – and they all took to the skies, the two-headed dog racing behind. Balthazar was left in an eerie silence.

Everything was quiet for what seemed like ages, then gentle sobs were heard coming from Wilfred. The kids ran over to him and wrapped him in the biggest hug, while the Sprites flew around him trying to console him. Even when the sound of the insects, birds and bugs returned, it was like they were trying to soothe him, too.

'Don't worry,' said Jimmy gently. 'I was told once, "The family is like an atom; split it at your peril" – well, we're a family and we're not going to let some evil witch just take our friends and get away with it! We'll get them back.'

'Course we will!' Billy said.

'Dear Wilfred,' Chief Mirren said, 'this certainly isn't the end – it is but the beginning. Have faith in the Rhythm, it has a plan for all of us.'

'Do you really believe that, Chief Mirren?' asked Jimmy nervously, struggling to see the positive in such a situation.

'I don't believe it, I *feel* it,' she replied. 'Anything that happens in this world and yours has been made possible because of the Rhythm. It often has a plan. You are all here now because the Rhythm wanted you to be. And as hard as it might feel, Bilfred and Andy being taken will be for a reason. Perhaps it means to put us in the right place so we can make a discovery that will right an imbalance, teach us something, help us to grow, or solve a problem for the Rhythm.'

'But I thought we fixed the problem with the Rhythm by exposing that horrible farm?' Anna said.

'The Rhythm is never completely safe,' Chief Mirren said. 'It must be looked after, and everybody and everything is responsible. The human world, it seems, has much to learn about that. I thought that stopping the pollution from your world to ours would be the answer to the recent feeling of the Rhythm being out of step, but perhaps that was just one small problem, not the whole. With the appearance of this red lady, I think something bigger is amiss and that's why the Rhythm called you all here.'

'Hang on, so are you saying the Rhythm got us to hug the tree in the first place?' asked Anna. 'That's blowing my mind a bit.'

'You, my friends, are the seeds of change,' Chief Mirren replied. 'With your different strengths and different ways of doing things, you have the tools to make a positive impact. We don't want hundreds of people who are all the same – they would all have the same way of doing things. By being unique, by simply being you, you bring so much more to life. That's why

82

I don't think it's luck that you three and Andy are here. You hold the key to the Rhythm's success.' Chief Mirren stopped for a minute and glanced at each of the children. 'I just don't know how yet.'

'And what about Scary Red and Terra Nova? What have they got to do with all of this?' Billy asked.

'If you're right that the lady in red is somehow in charge of Bilfred's garden, then my guess is that this Terra Nova is manipulating nature and taking what it shouldn't from these woods,' she replied seriously. 'And that can't carry on. But first things first, we have to save Bilfred and Andy.'

'We can go after them – maybe Rosemary and Cassia can help us, as they are such good trackers. They can follow the trail of saffron on Scary Red,' Billy suggested.

'Very well. While you're gone, we'll work together to repair Balthazar and get it battle-ready in case the red lady returns. This time we will be prepared,' Chief Mirren said. 'But be careful, children, she has shown herself to be very dangerous indeed.'

Billy gulped. Chief Mirren was right, this wasn't going to be safe. He looked at Jimmy and Anna. What if one of them got captured like Andy? He thought back to the climb up the waterfall and Anna's slip. He realized he couldn't bear the idea of her getting seriously hurt . . .

'Do you need someone to help you here?' he said quickly. 'Anna, why don't you stay? You're so good with the younger Sprites. They look up to you . . .'

Anna stared at Billy, her mouth wide open. 'What on earth are you talking about?' she said furiously. 'I want to go with you!'

He avoided her gaze. 'I just think you would be great here, you're so brilliant in a crisis,' Billy explained in a rush, not wanting to say the real reason he was suggesting she stay behind. 'And we don't all need to go . . . Jimmy and I can find Andy and then come back so we can work out a plan of what to do next.'

'Anna, we actually really could do with your help,' Chief Mirren said. 'Your strength of character is exactly what we need to prepare this place for another battle.'

Anna nodded reluctantly – she couldn't say no to Chief Mirren – but turned to Billy and gave him a look of daggers.

'I want to go after my brother,' Wilfred said. 'It sounded like she was going to take him straight back to his garden. I can't bear to leave him there alone.'

'I'll escort yous through the woods, Wilfred, sir,' Basil said. 'I knows where his garden is.'

'Thank you, Basil,' Chief Mirren said. 'That's a good idea. But you must come straight back when Wilfred and Bilfred are reunited. We need you here.'

It wasn't long before Billy and Jimmy had collected their stashed buzzpacks, while Cassia, Rosemary, Wilfred and Basil had gathered supplies and were ready to head out on their journeys.

'Bye, Anna. We'll see you soon,' Billy said.

'Back before you know it!' Jimmy added.

'I'm not talking to you,' Anna snapped back, then muttered under her breath, 'and you'd be back sooner with my help.'

'Anna, sometimes your friends' adventures aren't yours,' Chief Mirren said, floating to sit on the girl's shoulder. 'Trust that you're where you're meant to be.

Carry on down your own path. And believe that true friends only ever want what's best for you.'

'But what if they are wrong?' Anna asked. 'Billy thinks he's protecting me, but he should know that I can look after myself. I hate it when we fall out – it's not what best friends should do!'

'It's healthy to have tricky times, to not always see things the same way,' Chief Mirren said. 'Billy's heart is in the right place, even if he doesn't always say or do things in the right way.'

'I know,' Anna replied, softening. 'I know that pain can be the greatest teacher, I learnt that a long time ago.'

'Exactly – the trick in life is not to avoid inevitable pain, but to feel it and learn fast, so the pain is quick and you move forward. We only ever grow from these situations. But you already know that, don't you, Anna?' said Chief Mirren with a reassuring smile, before giving her the smallest hug.

Chapter 5

Back to Balance

High up in the sky, the Rangers and Scary Red rocketed towards the walled garden with Andy and Bilfred still firmly held as their prisoners. Soon enough, Bilfred's garden came into view and Scary Red instructed the group to land inside the walls.

Even the appearance of Scary Red and her Rangers in their home couldn't stop the insects and animals of the garden erupting with a joyous welcome for Bilfred – all kinds of whistles, croaks and buzzes filled the air, and the plants leant forward and puffed out wafts of pink and yellow pollen. They knew their heartbeat was home.

As frightened and sad as Bilfred was to be

captured again, he couldn't help but smile at the greeting. He'd loved being free, but he now realized he had missed his garden, too.

'Oh, hello, my little friends!' he said. 'How have you be–'

'Silence!' yelled Scary Red. Once again she rose and hovered in front of Bilfred's face, staring into his eyes. 'My best grower,' she said in a soft, condescending voice, 'you're back, and this time you will stay here – where you belong - *forever*. I remember when I first gave you this wonderful garden.' She extended her arms and looked around. 'Look at what I allowed you to have, and how do you choose to repay me? By abandoning your duties and putting *all* of us at risk. You're lucky I have decided to give you another chance.'

'You didn't give Bilfred anything,' Andy piped up from the ground. 'You *stole* his childhood! Made him a prisoner!'

'Silence!' Scary Red glared at Andy. 'This has nothing to do with you. Grower 162 understands what an honour it is to look after this garden. How lucky he

has been to work for Terra Nova.'

Bilfred looked at her, not knowing what to say. His heart was torn. He did love his garden, so, was she right? Was he wrong to have ever left it behind?

'Bilfred!' Andy cried, interrupting his thoughts. 'Don't listen to her! She trapped you here! She took you away from Wilfred!'

The Giant nodded his head. Andy was right. Scary Red was trying to make him forget what she had done. He cared about his garden, but he loved his brother and family more, and she had taken that from him for most of his life.

'My little friend is right,' Bilfred said defiantly. 'You didn't *give* me anything. You *took* from me. So you might have won for now, but my wonderful garden and I will be free of you. You mark my words.'

Scary Red laughed. 'Is that right? Well, if you leave again, I'll burn this garden to ashes. Everything. All your ickle, squirmy, wormy, feathery friends, will all BURN!' There was a moment's pause, then she said quietly, 'Dead garden . . .'

Bilfred's eyes widened. 'You wouldn't. You need this garden. You said so.'

'Did I?' Scary Red asked. 'No, Bilfred. I need *you*. This garden is only useful to me while you are in it. So without you . . .' she tailed off and looked around with a shrug. 'Do you *understand*?'

'Y . . . y . . . yes,' he stuttered with fright.

'I knew you'd come to your senses,' she said with a satisfied smile. 'Now get back to work! You're behind schedule with your deliveries, so you'll need to work doubly hard to make up for lost time.'

She raised her staff and the Rangers lifted into the air, one of them taking Andy by the waist.

'Grower 162 won't be any more trouble, so now we just need to deal with this,' she instructed, pointing at Andy. 'Back to base!'

'Where are you taking me?' Andy wailed. 'Police! Mum! Billyyyyyy!'

Bilfred watched helplessly as Scary Red and her Rangers disappeared with Andy into the distance, his arms and legs dangling in the air.

'Oh no, my friend, my Andy!' Bilfred mumbled to himself.

'Pssst!' came a noise from on top of the wall.

'Who's that?' Bilfred said, bewildered.

'It's Billy and Jimmy!' Billy whispered loudly, his head popping over the wall, closely followed by

Jimmy's. The boys hoisted themselves up and looked down at Bilfred. 'Cassia and Rosemary are here, too.' The two little Sprites popped up on the wall next to them, waving.

'I'm so glad you're here, but Scary Red's still got poor Andy!' Bilfred told them. 'I don't know where she's taken him.'

'Don't you worry. Leave Andy to us,' replied Billy.

'That's why Rosemary and I are here,' Cassia added. 'We're going to follow Scary Red's saffron trail and find out where she's taken Andy.'

'We knew she was going to bring you back to your garden,' Jimmy told Bilfred. 'And Basil is leading Wilfred here to be with you while we go and find Andy. They'll be here soon and will help work out a plan to set you free.'

Bilfred shook his head. 'I can't leave my garden again. She'll set fire to it and hurt all my friends!'

'We won't let her,' Jimmy said. 'She's not going to get away with this! We'll find out what she's really up to and put a stop to her plans. For now you just have to keep Scary Red happy by grow-grow-growing.'

'We can't let her know that we're plotting anything,' Billy continued. 'So get singing that lovely song of yours again, and we'll somehow save Andy without getting eaten or having our eyes sucked out, or being squashed by Rangers or anything else terrible we haven't thought about yet. Right, Jimmy?'

'Right, Billy. What would the summer holidays be without the risk of being vaporized by robots?' said Jimmy, rolling his eyes.

'Thank you, my friends. Wait, where's Anna?' Bilfred asked.

'Oh . . . she's back at Balthazar helping Chief Mirren and the Sprites,' Billy said. 'It was my suggestion, but she wasn't very happy. She gave me the look of death!'

'I'm not really surprised, Billy. It's not up to you to decide what Anna should be doing,' Jimmy said.

'Why would you stop her coming?' Bilfred said.

Billy looked bashful. 'I just wanted her to be safe. She nearly hurt herself earlier and Scary Red is dangerous! What if she somehow kidnapped Anna like she did you and Andy? Anna always jumps into things without thinking! I want to look after her,' Billy said.

Bilfred smiled. 'It's nice that you care about your friends – your heart, young Billy, is as big as one of my precious bazooka pumpkins. But Anna is brave and fierce and clever, and even though she might jump in head first where you like to make plans, that doesn't mean you're right and she's wrong. Or that she's right and you're wrong. It just means that you do things differently. If she's truly your friend, you've got to trust her. You're her pal, not her parent.'

Billy sighed. Bilfred was right. Anna didn't need him to tell her what to do, and he should have known that by now. 'Maybe I do owe her an apology,' he said.

Jimmy nodded. 'I think you do, Billy. But first we need to get cracking and find Andy, then we can head back to Balthazar and you can put on your apology pants!'

Bilfred chuckled. 'They are some BIG pants, Billy boy!'

'I can see the trail up ahead,' Cassia said, flitting up to the sky.

'We'll lead the way!' Rosemary said.

And, with a wave the four of them were off, flying through the air after Scary Red and her Rangers.

Now he knew there was a plan, Bilfred could relax a little and he fell to the ground, saying, 'Hello little ones. Oh, how I've missed you.' It wasn't long before he was enveloped by hundreds of colourful creatures giving him a welcome-home hug that made him look twice as big – swarms of bugs and murmurations of birds wafted around his head, while all kinds of animals did the most extraordinary dance

at his feet, and they all seemed to be humming his favourite song.

'Right, where are we? What have you been up to while I've been away?' he said to the creatures in the garden. 'What do you mean the beedleburps have swallowed all the bush fruit again? Honestly, I turn my back for five minutes. And what are you doing self-seeding over there? It was *not* my fault for leaving! I was following my dreams, following my brother. That's right, I found my long-lost brother – you know, the one I told you about! You want to hear the story? OK, well, where shall I begin . . . ?'

Chapter 6

Wandering Wilfred

Back in the woods, Wilfred and Basil were going as fast as the old man's legs would take him. (Which admittedly wasn't very fast, but it was progress nonetheless.)

'Don't you worries, Mr Revel, we'll get you backs to your brother in no times at all,' Basil said reassuringly.

'Oh, thank you, Basil,' Wilfred said, feeling braver with every step. 'I might be old, but slow and steady wins the race.'

'Don't say that Mr Revel,' Basil cried. 'We don't talk about trees getting older, they just grow, so it's the same for you. Now, I'm pretty sures I can gets yous into Bilfred's garden, but how we gets yous out is another matter.'

'I'm not worried about that,' Wilfred replied. 'As long as Bilfred is in the garden, I'll be there with him. Even if that means staying forever.'

'Do you knows how to grows, Mr Revel?' Basil quizzed.

'I have done my fair share of growing over the years,' Wilfred said. 'When Bilfred first went missing and I lost my eye, everyone was so nice to me and my family. They were always visiting, always around. But when everyone decided I had made the whole thing up, that stopped, and suddenly I was alone.'

'That's sads, Mr Revel,' said Basil. 'I hates to be alone.'

'I started spending more time in our garden. Actually, *all* the time. It was where I felt safe. And it was where I could keep an eye on the comings and goings in the woods, too, to stop anyone else from being taken.'

'Did yous not have any friends other than Bilfred?' Basil asked, wanting to keep Wilfred's mind from thinking about how far they were walking.

'I had a best friend. But I think he was told not to play with me any more when it all happened. So it was just me and Mum and Dad. Until it was just me and Mum. And then eventually it was just me.' Wilfred looked sad for a moment. 'But never mind that – I've got Bilfred back now. That's why I'm going to stay with him, no matter what.'

'You're rights,' Basil said. 'And the pasts is the pasts, and what's important is there's still laughters and joy to be had. None of us knows what's round the corner, but I've got a feelings – right here in my third eye on my foreheads – that you've gots a lot of loves to give and funs to have yet.'

Basil and Wilfred shared the warmest smile.

They hadn't gone much further into the woods when the strangest high-pitched squealing noise came from up ahead.

'What's that noise?' Wilfred said.

'I don't knows, Mr Revel,' said Basil.

Together they raced ahead, keeping a lookout for what could be making such an awful racket.

They hadn't gone far when they spotted a
baby Boona with its head and horns stuck
between two trees. It must've been there for
some time, because the fur around its neck
was all scuffed where it had been struggling
to get out.

'What on earth is that?' Wilfred asked.

'That, Mr Revel, is a Boona,' the Sprite said,
then he turned to the stuck creature. 'How longs
have you been stuck heres, then, my stinky friend?'

The Boona couldn't believe that someone had
come along. 'Three days I've been here. I didn't tell
any of my family where I was going, and I was
trying to get those fruits.' There, right in front
of the poor Boona, were four of the most
rainbow-bright, juicy, perfect buttonberries,
bursting with juiciness. They did look
good. 'That's what I was after. I leant
through and got stuck. I'm starving. I'm
so relieved you're here!'

'What's your name?' Wilfred
asked the small Boona.

100

'I'm Bovine Puffball Stinker. But everyone calls me Bo.'

'Ahh, it's nice to be named after a mushroom. They're full of vitamin D – good for your bones, good for your muscles, good for your brain!' said Wilfred.

'All us Boonas have a mushroom for a middle name. It's because it's our job in the Rhythm to spread the spores that grow into mushrooms and take care of the woods,' Bo explained proudly.

'Bo, I is Basil, and this is Mr Revel,' Basil said, introducing them. 'Right, let's get yous out of here, shall we's? Any ideas how, Mr Revel?'

Wilfred inspected the tree. 'The way I see it, we have two choices – cut the tree or cut the horn.' He pointed to the horn on Bo's head that was particularly wedged in.

'Cut my horn! It won't hurt,' the Boona replied quickly. 'The tree's too precious.'

'Good choices,' agreed Basil. And, with that, Wilfred pulled out his Swiss Army knife. It wasn't long before the horn was off and the Boona was free.

'Thank you ever so much. I never thought I would

be free and get to my fruit,' Bo said with delight, rubbing her scuffed head.

Wilfred reached into the bush to pick the fruits that had been teasing the stinker for the last three days. 'Here you go, Bo,' he said and popped a few straight into the Boona's mouth. She chomped and slurped with absolute joy, a big smile flashing over her face as she made all the usual excitable noises plus a few Boona grunts – 'Eademup yum-yum.'

Wilfred, Basil and Bo took a moment to drink water from the stream and pick a few wild fruits. Then, after they'd had a little rest, it was time for Basil and Wilfred to keep going.

'Well, nice to meet you, Bo, but we have to be on our way. My brother is waiting,' Wilfred said, giving Bo a scratch under her chin.

'Bye, then,' Bo replied, looking sadly at the pair as they walked away.

Basil and Wilfred had only been walking for a short time when they heard a scampering behind them. They turned around and – lo and behold – it was little Bo bounding down the path.

'What are you doing back so fast?' Wilfred asked.

'Um . . .' she said as she caught up to them. 'Well, I thought that it might be . . . ummm . . . helpful for me to spend more time with Andy the Weapon's elders. So I wondered if I could come with you? In the name of research, o' course,' Bo asked, looking up hopefully.

'Don't you thinks you should gets back to your family? What if they thinks we've kidnapped yous?' Basil said. 'I don't wants to start nos trouble with the Stinkers!'

'They won't come looking for me. I had an argument with my auntie, because they all eat anything and everything and I only want to eat fruit and veg and seeds and nuts,' Bo said with a shrug. 'That's why I was stuck for so long. They banished me.'

Basil and Wilfred looked at each other and shared a nod. 'Why not, the more the merrier,' Wilfred said.

They walked on together. Every now and again, Bo would stop to forage for something for them to eat. She even found them drinks, too, in the form of beautiful cup-shaped white flowers full of fresh dew water that had the scent of home-made lemonade.

'I'm very pleased that you've joined our journey,' Wilfred said as she handed them the cups, and Bo beamed with pride.

After a couple of hours, the trees cleared and they came face to face with an enormous wall.

'I tolds you we'ds get you backs together again,' said Basil triumphantly. 'Just one last little hurdle to overcomes.'

'A little hurdle?' Wilfred exclaimed, staring up at the giant wall blocking their way.

'Hmmmm. You're right. Hows on earth are we's going to get yous in, Mr Revel?' Basil said. 'I can fly, but I can't carry a grown hooman like you. Not alone.'

They looked around, hoping to find an answer.

Basil pointed to some tall trees at the edge of the wall. 'Can yous get up those, Mr Revel? I think that's how the kids got in when they first found Bilfred.'

'I can give it a try . . .' Wilfred replied, sounding nervous. 'I haven't climbed a tree for years. I don't know if I've got it in me any more.'

'Well, I's never had to, o' course, but I remember Anna sayings to the others that yous want to look for a tree thats branches looks like steps and then, before yous knows it, you'll be sky-high,' Basil offered.

Wilfred scanned the nearby trees for the best option. He reached out and took a first couple of tentative, shaky steps. He gulped, but kept going, and, gripping super tightly, managed to get a bit higher.

'Yous doings ever so wells, Mr Revel,' said Basil encouragingly, zipping up beside him. 'Remember, no lookings down, only looks up. The only ways is up.'

Wilfred took a deep breath and kept climbing, his face breaking into a smile as he reached the top of the wall and finally caught a glimpse of his brother.

Wilfred then clambered on to the top and there he sat with Basil, watching Bilfred in the midst of his eccentric, extravagant choreography, flipping, flopping, burping and bopping around the garden.

Wilfred gave a round of applause. 'Brother,' he cried happily from his wall-top perch, 'I'm here!'

At the sound of his brother's voice, Bilfred bounded over. 'I'm so pleased to see you,' he said, jumping up and down.

'Yes, I'm here!' Wilfred beamed. 'Basil brought me, and I made a new friend on the way!' He looked around on the ground outside the wall, but there was no sight of Bo. Where had she gone?

'Jump down and I'll catch you,' Bilfred told his brother.

Wilfred nodded, and with complete faith, he jumped off the high wall. Bilfred caught him effortlessly.

Basil flew over and landed on Bilfred's shoulder. And before they could even wonder where Bo was, the clumsy bumble of stinking joy casually wandered over to them.

'Hows did yous gets in, little Boona?' Basil asked in surprise.

'I just used the door over there,' Bo replied, pointing to the small red door on the other side of the garden.

'Oh, yes!' said Bilfred. 'That was very sensible.'

'There's a door?' asked Wilfred. He looked at Basil. 'Why on earth didn't you say?'

'I didn't knows!' Basil said.

'It's much too small for you, my brother,' said Bilfred reassuringly, with a wink towards Basil. 'It was even a bit of a stretch for the kids to get through.'

'Wow! Is that ALL compost?' Bo cried. She thundered towards a giant heap, taking a flying leap into the air and diving head first into the stinking pile. Every so often she came up for air, but she was having so much fun scrabbling around in the twigs and leaves, making friends with the insects and creatures that lived in it. It was clear to all that Bo was loving life.

'Right, well, nows that I've got yous here safely, Mr Revel,' Basil said, 'I needs to go back to Balthazar.' He zipped up into the air with a wave. 'We'll come up with a plan to free you forever, Bilfred. You waits and sees!'

The brothers waved as Basil vanished over the side of the wall, then they turned their attention to the garden.

'Billy and Jimmy were here and went off following Scary Red,' Bilfred told his brother. 'They said that for now I've got to pretend things have gone back to normal. So I've got to get this garden back to firing on all cylinders, so she doesn't come back for a good long while.'

'I'm worried about the kids,' Wilfred said, frowning. 'I don't know what they're going to get themselves into.'

'The one thing I know about Billy, Jimmy, Anna and Andy is that together they can do anything. They'll come up with a plan – we have to trust them. And we have to do what they've said. Normal is what Scary Red wants, so, once the growing is back on track, then we can decide what to do next. Although . . .' Bilfred trailed off.

'What is it?' Wilfred asked.

'Being back here has made me remember how much I love this garden,' Bilfred admitted. 'I want to live here, but I don't want to be trapped any more.'

'Well, perhaps there's a way to do just that,' Wilfred suggested. He looked at the tiny red door in the wall. 'We're just going to need a bigger door . . .'

Bilfred smiled. 'Since that awful day I lost you, I've been locked in this garden, all on my own,

with no other humans, for over fifty years – well, until Billy and the gang came along. Without my garden friends, I would have been lost.'

'I suppose I've hardly spoken to anyone for fifty years either. No one wanted to be near me, and it felt pretty hopeless at times. I've been so lonely.' He looked up at Bilfred in his garden home and smiled sadly. 'I'm glad you weren't so hopeless, Bilfred. That you found peace in this garden.'

'You're right,' Bilfred confirmed. 'I was very upset, o' course, but I have been able to bond with nature like I never even imagined. And now I get to share it with you, which is even better.'

He made a few clicking sounds and a family of lizards came over and seemed to click in response.

'D . . . did you just talk to that lizard? How?' Wilfred asked in awe.

'Now that is a question,' said Bilfred. 'I can't explain, you just have to feel it, and that takes a bit of time and focus. These lizards talk through a mixture of smells and vibrations and nods and things. I've been here so long now, I've got it down pat – a nod means yes, and when they are not happy or they are angry you can smell it. But most of their communication comes from vibrations. The lizards were the first to get chatty with me when I was a kid. The birds were next.'

'When you say you have to feel it – feel what?' Wilfred asked.

Bilfred held up his arm and pointed at the little hairs, then nodded at the lizard.

'There,' he said to Wilfred. 'My hairs moved – did you see?'

Wilfred was still confused. 'You mean you just spoke to the lizard through the hairs on your arm? Well, what did it say?'

'He said it's nice to meet you! He can definitely see the family resemblance, although you're a lot shorter, and I'm afraid he said you don't smell as sweet as me.' Bilfred chuckled.

'You got all of that from a little movement in your arm hair?'

'I did. And you get used to nature's vibrations. If you speed up a human voice, it sounds like a bird;

if you speed up a bird, it sounds like an insect – and
if you slow them all down, it sounds like a fish. It's
all just sound waves. You just have to be able to
speed up or slow down your hearing, and that simply
requires time and meditation. Although, I have to say,
the hardest but most important vibration of all to pick
up was the Myas.'

'The Myas?' asked Wilfred, mesmerized.

'The Myas are the mycelium,' Bilfred explained.
'They're everywhere, even on our skin – but under the
ground they interconnect all the trees, sometimes
hundreds of miles away. I like to call them the world
wood web of communication!'

With that, Bilfred stretched out his fingers and
sunk them into the soil. He closed his eyes, took a big
deep breath and held it there for a moment, then
slowly breathed out and started to nod.

'They're parched, poor things. The mycelium, from
a mile away near the river, has been sending them
just enough water to keep them alive, but they haven't
had a good drink in ages.' Then he picked up the
pearly white stone that hung around his neck and

looked through the hole to see the weather.
'But I can see that there's a storm
just around the corner – lots of
rain is coming!'

'Do you have a stone
that can tell if food is on
its way?' asked Wilfred, 'Cos
I'm starving!'

Bilfred let out a hearty
laugh. He darted into the shed and came
out with a jar of biscuits.

'Ooh, I do love a digestive,' said Wilfred eagerly.

'It's not a biscuit, oh no – watch this!' Bilfred
poured water over a couple of them. As they
rehydrated, they puffed up and quadrupled in size,
transforming from dry, gnarly looking things into soft
spongy cakes. He drizzled over a little honey and
sprinkled on little flavoursome balls that popped in
your mouth. At the sight of food, Bo bounded over and
joined the brothers.

'Do you want a cake, Bo?' Bilfred asked.

'Er, actually, I've been eyeing up those pumpkins

over there,' said Bo, and she galloped over and started tucking into the orange flesh, saying over and over, 'Eademup yum-yum, eademup yum-yum!'

Now that he'd properly stopped, Wilfred was feeling tired.

'You put your feet up, Wilfred,' said Bilfred, seeing his brother's eyelids drooping. 'I'll start getting everything in balance again.'

So as Wilfred snoozed, Bilfred shifted and organized the garden in the most beautiful way. He cut back the roses and a huge selection of different flowers that he'd planted next to the veg patch to keep away certain types of bugs and attract others to help pollinate the plants.

In the corner of the garden was a set of pipes that Bilfred had designed to fit into different positions, creating a complex yet effective watering system. With just the twist of a pipe, water dripped, sprayed or gushed wherever it was needed. As Bilfred pumped water into his garden, a calm fell over everything as the plants took a breath to drink up the goodness. You could almost see the colour in everything start to glow again, and the birds and bugs bathed in the mists.

However, in one corner, a swarm of bees seemed visibly annoyed at the spray of water. Bilfred went over and broke into the most extraordinary set of movements and spins, like a very wacky dance.

'What are you doing?' Bo asked, scampering over.

'I'm talking to the bees,' said Bilfred. 'I know they don't like the water, but they like the nectar, and you can't have one without the other.' He jumped into the air and did a big windmill move with his arms, and, with that, the bees calmly went back into the hive.

'I think we're getting there,' Bilfred said, looking around with satisfaction.

Bo leapt over to Wilfred, jumping up on the old man and stirring him from sleep.

'Look at the garden, Mr Revel!' she said. 'Isn't it lovely?'

Wilfred nodded and smiled with pride at the paradise his brother had nurtured.

'Now that you're awake, shall we have something a bit more substantial than cake?' Bilfred suggested. 'How about a grisotto?'

'A what?' asked Wilfred.

'A grisotto. It's one of my favourite garden recipes. I cut a pumpkin in half and put it on the fire so the outside burns, but the inside goes sweet and soft. Then I stir that through grains from the edge of the garden. Oh, I think I might even still have a bit of salted cheese in the shed . . .'

He ran into the shed and came out triumphant,

holding a block of cheese, as well as all the ingredients needed to make the food.

'Wilfred, can you pick some wild flowering oregano, marjoram and sage – they're all over there? They'll flavour the dish beautifully.' Wilfred followed his brother's instructions and came back with a handful of fragrant leaves.

'Do you want an orange grisotto or a green one?' Bilfred asked.

'Green?' shrugged Wilfred.

'Right then, you smash those herb leaves into mush,' Bilfred instructed. Once ready, Bilfred stirred in the herbs, turning the orange, gloopy, starchy, comforting grisotto the most brilliantly vibrant green. He poured it into carved wooden bowls, then used a knife to nick out little pearly chunks of cheese, which snowed down on to the sea of green. Bilfred added some zukabazooka huckleberries on the side, then, before Wilfred could tuck in, he let out a high-pitched whistle and looked across the garden. Out of nowhere, a shower of tiny yellow and mauve petals rained down over the bowls. Bilfred winked. 'The finishing touch!

They're very mustardy, very nice.'

As they tucked in, Wilfred's eyes widened. 'Ooooohh! That is good.'

Then Bilfred jumped up. 'Oh no! I've forgotten my special apple juice! Hang on, it's the perfect drink to have with this.' Another trip to the shed and he came back with a big jug and poured the special apple juice into metal tankards.

Wilfred took a sip and announced, 'This is cider!'

'No, it's not, it's my special apple juice. I don't know what cider is.'

'Well, it's special apple juice!'

They carried on eating and drinking to their hearts' content, laughing as they exchanged stories and memories from both sides of the woods and the walled garden.

Deep down, neither had forgotten the danger that lurked beyond the walls, but for just a short snippet of time, things seemed perfect as the brothers celebrated being together once more.

Chapter 7

Code Red

Andy had tried to keep track of where they were going as he was flown across the woods, but it had been impossible. He just hoped his friends would have some kind of plan to find him, because he didn't think he would ever be able to find his way back to Balthazar or the entrance to Waterfall Woods.

He had been taken to an impressive compound that sat in a clearing surrounded by forest. The sound of a waterfall thundered nearby and, through the trees, Andy glimpsed a river leading to a cliff edge.

The building itself was an extraordinarily grey, angular, almost beautifully ugly thing that looked totally out of place amid the lush greenery of the forest. And

yet it was nestled so snugly in the landscape, with trees and plants growing around it, that it also looked like it had always been there. However, there was no doubt the woods were angry that it had intruded where it wasn't welcome. *This must be where she lives*, Andy thought to himself

Inside, it was just as futuristic as it was on the outside. Huge windows looked out on to every possible view of the woods that surrounded the building.

Andy was taken down to a dark and dingy cell in the basement. But, as Scary Red threw him inside, suddenly the house wasn't the most surprising thing; it was that he wasn't the only eleven-year-old boy there . . . Bruno Brace, the school bully who had caused Billy a fair amount of trouble, was already inside, quivering in the corner.

'I haven't got time for this,' Scary Red said, her voice full of annoyance. 'I can't use either of you as growers; you're too old. And I can't let you go because you know too much. But I am curious as to how you arrived here . . . I'll just have to think about what to do with you. I'll be back soon.' And she swished out of the automatic door, which locked itself behind her.

'Bruno!' said Andy. 'What are you doing here?'

'N-n-no, this is a big mistake,' stammered Bruno. 'This wasn't part of the plan. It's all your fault!'

'My fault?' Andy snapped back.

'Well, I followed you, didn't I, and now I'm trapped in this weird basement!'

'You followed me?' Andy said, surprised and slightly annoyed.

'Yeah, I saw you on your bike, making the police and their dogs chase you, and wanted to know what you were up to. Then you ran into the woods, so I followed you. I figured at the very least I could steal your pocket money, and your mates', too. But then you hugged that big tree and vanished!' Bruno took a deep breath and let out a heavy sigh. 'I tried copying you – you best not tell anyone about me hugging trees! – and you appeared from nowhere, heading off into the woods. I followed, and that's when I got caught by a flying robot thing. It flew me to THIS horrible place and THAT horrible woman.'

'Well, that just shows you shouldn't follow people

and try to steal their pocket money,' huffed Andy.

'Never mind that! What is this place? Where are we?' Bruno asked, his voice rising. 'And why don't you seem as freaked out about all this as I am?'

'Would you like a perfect cheese toastie?' Andy asked calmly.

'What?!'

'I mean, obviously it's better to use a toaster or a grill,' Andy explained, 'but if you've got the patience, beautiful things can happen with your own body heat – thirty-seven degrees is just hot enough to make the cheese go oozy.'

Bruno looked on, totally speechless, as Andy removed a foil-wrapped parcel from his trousers, and he continued to stare in horror as Andy unwrapped the foil to reveal what – Bruno hated to admit – looked like a really delicious toastie, even if it was moulded beautifully into the shape of Andy's bum cheeks!

'I just place it between my buttocks to warm it up and keep the shape,' Andy continued with pride. 'A couple of hours and it's good to go! Look, I admit it's unconventional, but it's resourceful, and as I was making lovely sarnies to lure the police dogs away, I made this extra special one for me in case of emergencies. Just look at this . . .'

Andy tore it apart – showing off a fondue of oozy cheeses, complete with red splodges of ketchup. He took a big satisfying bite, then held out the other half to Bruno. 'It's mostly Cheddar and Red Leicester. And the trick for the ultimate stringy ooze is a little slice of Swiss cheese. Want some? It has been wrapped in foil, so it's, you know, safe.'

Bruno was still in shock. 'That's disgusting! And this is no time to eat!'

'Ahh, it's never a bad time to eat, Bruno,' Andy said, rubbing his belly. 'Mum says I've got ABS –

that's angry bowel syndrome. The doctors said my tummy doesn't like bread. It makes it very gurgly, shall we say. So right now, me eating a cheese toastie might even help get us out of here . . .'

Bruno sighed. He didn't know what to think, or what was going on, but . . . it had been ages since he'd eaten anything. Before he could change his mind, he grabbed the half Andy offered him and took a bite.

'Mmmm,' Bruno mumbled through a mouthful. 'That's good!' He tucked into the delicious toastie with gusto, enjoying the ooziness of the cheese combo.

'You like the crushed beef-and-onion crisps I added as a final touch? It gives it a whole new level of flavour,' Andy said proudly. Then he took a deep breath. 'Right, let's fire up "the weapon".'

Bruno raised an eyebrow, confused by Andy's chat. 'What's the weapon?' he asked through a mouthful of toastie.

'You'll find out . . . I give it about six minutes, and I'll be ready to blow,' Andy explained, massaging his tummy.

'Oh no,' whimpered Bruno.

Andy nodded and glanced at the ceiling. 'It looks like there's a sprinkler system in here, so there must also be a smoke detector. I reckon that it will never have detected anything like this before,' he said, pointing proudly at his bottom. 'And if we can get Scary Red back here, then maybe I can take her breath away, too.'

'HEY!' Bruno yelled. 'HEY . . . LADY!'

'OI!' Andy joined in, catching on to Bruno's idea. 'YOU CAN'T LEAVE US HERE! LET US OUT!'

'YEAH! LET US OUT! LET US OUT!' Bruno shouted.

'LET US OUT! LET US OUT! LET US OUT!' the boys cried together. 'LET US –'

Red came flying back into the room.

'SILENCE! Why are you making so much noise! And what is that dis-GUSTING smell? What on earth are you doing in here?'

'We're just sharing a cheese toastie – want some?' Andy replied innocently, with a wink.

Red looked utterly disgusted. 'Food is forbidden in my house! The State gives all the people of Terra Nova perfect nutrition in a vial, so we don't waste precious time and energy cooking and eating. This behaviour is for simpletons.' And she retched at the thought.'

Andy and Bruno looked at each other, puzzled, then the penny dropped. 'Don't you miss the taste of a good sarnie? Or a roast dinner? Or a fresh smoothie? Or a spaghetti Bolognese? Or a jam doughnut?' said Andy, as he patted his bubbling tummy and signalled to Bruno that they needed to keep the lady talking.

Bruno jumped in with, 'What about a doner kebab, heavy on the chilli?'

'Or a chicken and sweetcorn pie with home-made crumbly pastry?' added Andy.

With every suggestion Scary Red gagged and went paler and paler. 'What are you talking about, you disgusting children,' Red said, sounding more and more frustrated.

'Oooh, beautiful barbecued spare ribs,' offered Bruno, getting into his stride. 'Or a nice chicken tikka masala. Or sweet and sour pork and pineapple, delicious!'

Andy's tummy rumbled and gurgled loudly.

Bruno was running out of ideas. 'Errrrr, I know, how about a nice trifle with blancmange, vanilla cream, clementine jelly and broken up chocolate flakes.'

'I'm starting to wish I'd fed you to the dog,' she replied.

'My nan's lasagne!' Bruno cried. 'Lots of lovely layers of mince and –'

PHWARRRRRUGHFFFFFFF!

Andy unleashed angriest beast he'd ever created: the biggest, most explosive, outrageous, volatile fart, that sounded like a whale's mating call.

Bruno's face rippled with the change of air pressure in the room, and Scary Red

was blown against the wall by the force.

Andy's suspicion about the sprinkler system was right, as the fire alarm was triggered and water burst from the sprinklers. To the boys' delight, the door to the room also sprang open.

'Andy, you're a genius,' Bruno cried, as they bolted for the door. They ran as fast as they could down the corridor and towards the stairs. They bounded up them two at a time, their legs working as hard as they could. But, as they got to the top, two Rangers appeared, blocking their way. They picked up the boys by the scruff of their necks and took them back down the corridor to the basement.

'ARGHHH! How DARE you try to escape,' Scary Red hissed,

holding her nose, as the Rangers threw them back inside. 'You'll pay for this insolence!'

There was a loud bleeping sound, and she looked down at what seemed to be a watch on her wrist.

'I will be back to punish you,' she sneered at Andy and Bruno, before storming off, the automatic door slamming shut.

'Well, that was one big fat failure!' whined Bruno.

'At least I tried something,' replied Andy, who was still out of breath from the effort and getting 'contractions' from the epic fart.

'I don't see you coming up with any bright ideas. I think if there's any chance of us escaping, we'll have to work together as a team. Truce?'

'Truce,' Bruno agreed. 'Just until we're out of here anyway,' he added.

Chapter 8
I'm Still Beautiful

Outside, Billy, Jimmy, Rosemary and Cassia had just arrived at the house, having followed the saffron tracks left by Scary Red. The boys stashed their buzzpacks in a nearby bush, ready to be grabbed if they needed to make a quick escape, then they crouched by a corner of the building, trying to stay out of sight.

'I think I can hear voices coming from inside,' Billy whispered.

'If Scary Red's in there, then Andy will be, too. We need to find a way inside to rescue him,' Jimmy said.

'Rosemary, Cassia, do you think you could find us an open window, or an unlocked door – something we can go through?' Billy asked the two Sprites.

'Sure we can, Billy,' Rosemary replied, and, with that, the two Sprites flitted off.

It wasn't long before they were back. 'We found a window!' Cassia announced. 'Follow us.'

Cassia and Rosemary sped off again, with Billy and Jimmy following. They ran after the Sprites until they reached a small window that was ajar on the ground floor.

'Thank you so much for getting us here; we couldn't have done this without you. You truly are the best trackers and finders,' Billy said to the Sprites. 'We'll take it from here. You go back to Balthazar and tell Chief Mirren that I'll send a message on the flint as soon as we find out what's going on inside this building.'

'Are you sure?' Cassia asked.

'Yes, we've got this, one hundred per cent.' Billy took a deep breath and smiled as the Sprites gave him and Jimmy a lovely little nose hug, before flitting off.

'Be careful,' Rosemary warned as they flew away. 'That red lady is dangerous!'

Billy and Jimmy looked at each other with apprehension.

'Ready?' Billy said.

'Ready,' Jimmy replied, nodding firmly. 'Let's go get our friend back!'

Billy pushed open the window and crawled through into the house, with Jimmy hot on his heels. They found themselves in a sparse, shiny white room. There were no pictures on the walls, no rugs on the floor, no signs of anything personal at all, apart from a few carefully placed objects on stone tables. In the centre of the room was a perfectly square white rock, and three red sculptures stood at the back of the room, all

in beautifully different shapes. It was stark but somehow beautiful.

'Gosh, I'm not sure what my mum would make of this,' Jimmy whispered. 'There's nothing sentimental here. Where are all the memories and the signs of good times?'

'I'm not sure Scary Red would have family photos on the wall. I wonder if she even has a family,' Billy whispered back. 'What kind of person has a beautiful vase with no flowers in it, when you live in the middle of a wood full of amazing plants?'

Billy turned to look and his backpack accidentally knocked the glass vase off its stone table. Luckily Jimmy managed to dive to catch it, just before it smashed on the floor.

'Nice save,' Billy said. 'I don't even know what this room is. A lounge? A dining room? There's nothing in here to give us any clues. But Andy's clearly not here. Come on, let's start looking around.'

They snuck quietly out of the room and down the corridor. The walls were white here, too, but they jutted out at all kinds of angles, creating an optical illusion of the corridor getting smaller the further you walked down it. Lights bounced in from behind the walls as the boys moved down the corridor. If they sped up, the lights sped up, too. Every now and then there'd be a sharp turn – it was almost like being in a maze.

'Wait, I've got something that might help us out,' Billy said, rummaging in his backpack. He pulled out an Etch A Sketch that he'd customized to help track paths by marking them with his finger. 'I thought this would come in handy when we explored the woods over the summer, but it seems like it's going to make sure we don't get lost in the weirdest house ever.'

'Clever, really clever,' Jimmy whispered in appreciation.

They continued on, Billy tracing their route on the Etch A Sketch as they went.

Suddenly, they froze in fear at the sound of a piercing scream. Scary Red. And she was really close.

They heard footsteps coming towards them, angrily stomping along. They looked at each other, preparing to run, but then the footsteps started to sound like they were heading in a different direction. Billy tiptoed forward and peered round the next corner. The corridor was empty, but a door was open – that had to be where she'd gone.

Billy wanted to run away, but he reminded himself that Andy needed them! So he motioned to Jimmy that they should keep going, and they carefully crept round the corner and towards the open door. As they drew close, Billy saw it had the word 'Canteen' written on it. Billy and Jimmy peeped inside, making sure they didn't make a sound – it didn't look anything like the school canteen they were used to. There were no tables and chairs, no drawers and cupboards for cutlery and cups, and no sign of any nearby kitchen to cook anything. It was just another bare white room, with a large mirror on one wall.

Billy was confused. *Why was this room called the canteen when there was no sign of any food?*

They watched as Scary Red stood in the middle of the room and waved her hand in mid-air. Billy held in a gasp as an illuminated marble cabinet slowly rose up from the floor in front of her. The doors opened to reveal rows of labelled glass vials, all full of brightly coloured liquids. To get a better view, Billy pulled out a periscope from his backpack – the labels were dated, with the wording: Nutrition Perfection.

Scary Red picked out a vial and held it up to the light. The orange liquid glimmered with sparkling flecks, and the lady smiled. She pulled open a gap in her dress to reveal her belly button, and Billy's eyes widened as he saw it was edged in gold and set with coloured jewels. She pushed the vial straight into the centre of her belly button and gently twisted it. The little glass tube became illuminated and the liquid

inside started to spin like a whirlpool. Scary Red took a deep breath in, closed her eyes, and then breathed out. The boys watched in horror as the liquid started to disappear into her belly button.

The air next to her suddenly lit up with a collection of words that looked like a neon sign:

Energy efficiency
Vitamin levels
Blood oxygen

Numbers and percentages flickered and changed beside the words.

An outline of a body appeared alongside the words, shaded in red, and then a graphic shaped like the vial appeared in orange. Slowly the body changed from red to amber to green, while the digital vial emptied. Scary Red's energy efficiency percentages increased from sixty-seven per cent up to ninety-eight per cent, and her other levels rose to one hundred per cent.

Billy nudged Jimmy as a timer on the wall started

to spin round and round before starting a countdown:

23 hours, 59 seconds . . .

23 hours, 58 seconds . . .

23 hours, 57 seconds . . .

'Do you think that countdown clock means she must do this every twenty-four hours?' Jimmy said as quietly as he could.

Billy nodded. 'And I'm not sure this 'canteen' has anything to do with food – it looks like she's getting everything she needs from that tiny vial.'

Scary Red opened her eyes, unclicked the vial from her belly button and replaced it in the cabinet, which then closed itself and sank back into the floor. She waved her hand again, and a smaller cabinet rose from the floor. This one opened to reveal a single bottle, labelled Youth-In-A-Bottle. It was a much smaller, fatter tube, with silver-speckled red liquid. Scary Red's face lit up with excitement and she took it out and gazed at it in wonder, before plugging it into her tummy.

Once again, the liquid started to disappear, as coloured lasers tracked over her face and body. Now the words **VISUAL AGE** were projected into the air.

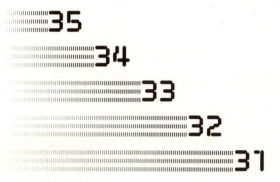

The boys watched on as the numbers fell until they stopped at twenty-five. With each change of number, the skin on the woman's face grew visibly tighter, dewier and more radiant.

'She's getting younger!' Billy hissed at Jimmy.

The vial empty, Scary Red removed it from her belly button and placed it back in the cabinet, which then whooshed back into the floor.

She moved closer to a mirror towards the back of the room, stroking her skin with a smile. Billy felt the hairs on his arms prickle with fear as Scary Red began to sing to herself in a haunting voice:

I steal children
　　To look young forever

Paid with youth in a bottle
　　Or I'll wrinkle and wither

A child for perfection
　　The price for complexion

My age, my obsession
My fire, my aggression

No guilt, no shame
No one to blame
But me

I'm shallow on the inside
I'm empty and cold
I'm ugly on the inside
But I'll never grow old

Cos I'm still beautiful
I'm still beautiful
I'm still beautiful
I'm still beautiful
I'm still beautiful
I'm still beautiful

I'm still beautiful
I'm still beautiful
I'm still beautiful

I'm still beautiful
I'm still beautiful

The eerie yet enchanting sound of Scary Red's song filled the air, sending shivers down Billy's and Jimmy's spines.

'I think we should get out of here while we can, she's clearly evil' Billy whispered.

They crept quietly away, Billy using the Etch A Sketch map to get them back to the white room that they'd originally entered.

'Phew, that was close!' Billy said as the door whooshed shut behind them. 'What on earth is going on? It's like Scary Red is from the future or something. But how is she here in the woods?'

'Never mind how she's here,' Jimmy said, looking worried. 'Billy, did you hear that song? She *has* to be the woman who took Bilfred all those years ago. And somehow those vials are keeping her young. Who knows how! I really don't like this; we need to find Andy and get back to Balthazar as fast as we can.'

The sound of footsteps echoed in the corridor outside.

'She's coming!' Billy cried. 'Hide!'

They dived behind the red sculptures, hearts

racing. Seconds later, the door swished open and Scary Red stormed in. She strode to the square structure in the centre of the room and waved her hand over it: another air projection appeared with words and numbers and flashing colours. Billy frantically tried to read them, but his brain was spinning, making it even harder for him to concentrate. He tried to slow his breathing and focus, but the letters still seemed to jump around in front of him. It was no good. As much as he hated to admit it, if they were going to figure this out, he was going to have to ask his friend to help.

'What does it say, Jimmy?' he whispered, his voice as low as possible.

'"Current growers: 303. Minimum required growers: 304. Reduction in output imminent. Address immediately!" – and that last part is flashing red, so it must be bad. What do you think it means?'

Billy's mind raced. Scary Red had called Bilfred Grower 162, and they knew from the map they had found in Balthazar that there were more gardens in Waterfall Woods . . . but surely this couldn't mean there were *303* gardens in Waterfall Woods?

Or 303 stolen children like Bilfred?

Scary Red waved her hand again, and the projection changed to show a photo of what looked like a Giant. Next to it words and numbers appeared. She flicked her hand and the image changed at speed, with photo after photo appearing. Billy tried again to make sense of it, but the letters just wouldn't come together. He tutted in frustration under his breath.

'It's like Top Trumps cards,' Jimmy whispered. 'Listing growers with stuff like flags of the nationalities of where they're from, how long they've been a grower, productivity . . .'

'Jimmy,' Billy whispered, eyes wide. 'What if these are ALL growers like Bilfred? That would mean she's got a whole production line going!'

Scary Red let out a sigh of displeasure and raised her hand again. A staff flew from the corner of the room into her hand, and she tapped it on the floor. Two Rangers raced into the room.

'Grower 162 has been returned to his garden,' Scary Red said. 'So why does the record still show that we have a missing grower?'

I'm Still Beautiful

'Grower 009 has passed,' a Ranger replied.

The woman glared at the Ranger. 'Name? Age?'

'Helga. 160 years, four months and two days,' the Ranger answered.

'Helga is one of our oldest growers.' Scary Red looked thoughtful. 'She was very productive indeed. It's a shame the State can't provide Youth-In-A-Bottle for all my growers. Though, I suppose, it is best reserved for important people. So now we have another problem that I have to deal with,' she raged.

'One of the first growers she stole was 160 years ago?' Billy whispered to Jimmy, horrified. They'd worked out that Scary Red was *much* older than she looked, but could she really be hundreds of years old?

'I need to find another grower of 009's quality. If only those *disgusting* boys in the basement were a bit younger. But they are useless! Too old to properly connect with the Rhythm in the gardens.'

With the flick of her wrist, Scary Red changed the projection in front of her. This time, Billy didn't need Jimmy's help to understand what it said. An image of

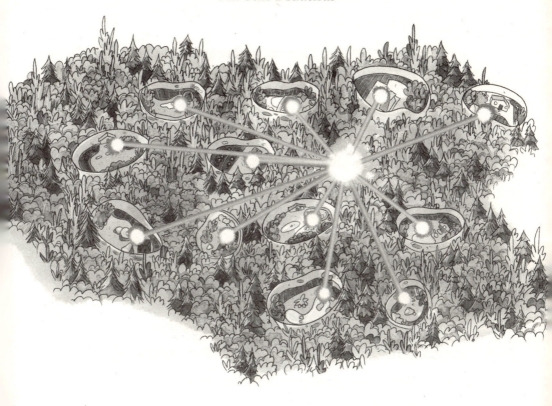

a map of Waterfall Woods hovered in the air, but it
was much bigger than he could ever have imagined.
There were hundreds of walled gardens scattered
deep in the woods, each with a flashing dot that Billy
guessed was a Giant grower like Bilfred. It was clear
now that Scary Red's operation was huge!

'Who are the most productive growers?' Red asked
aloud.

149

More stats and photos immediately flashed up –
Billy noticed a picture of a woman with the name
'Helga' underneath it.

'Hmmm, I need to go to Australia – that country
has consistently given me some excellent growers,'
Scary Red said.

She motioned to one of the Rangers. 'You, please
ensure you and your team go about the daily pick-ups
as usual. I'm going to find a new grower before the
State notices anything more is amiss. I'll be back
before the end of the day, so please use this
opportunity to recharge and reboot and make sure all
your systems are updated from the State's
supercomputer.'

With a swipe of her watch, her dress changed into
a smart red suit, complete with matching bumbag.
'Awesome!' she said in an Australian accent.

The boys watched as she walked outside and let
out a blood-curdling howl. The horrendous sound was
immediately echoed back to her by her Death Hound.
Billy and Jimmy were pleased they were well hidden
from sight.

'Over 300 growers! All stolen children from all over the world,' Jimmy said when the coast was clear.

'And it proves Scary Red must be really old. I wonder what would happen if she didn't take that Youth-In-A-Bottle? I bet she'd shrivel up like a prune,' Billy said.

'Did you notice she said, "*boys* in the basement"?' Jimmy asked. 'We know that Andy is here, but who else has she kidnapped?'

'I don't know . . .' Billy said. 'Let's go and find out.'

'Yes, once we've rescued Andy – and whoever he's with – then we can work out how we can help the growers, these lost children.'

As they crept out from their hiding place, Billy saw a flash of movement outside. Then the face of someone who definitely shouldn't have been there appeared at the window . . .

'Anna!' Billy cried. He and Jimmy ran over to the window and climbed back outside. Jimmy gave Anna a hug, but when Billy went to do the same, she stepped aside, her face looking furious.

'I'm not happy with you,' Anna told him. 'You left

me in Balthazar when you knew I wanted to be here with you.'

Billy looked down, ashamed. 'I just wanted to keep you safe,' he said. 'And sometimes, well, sometimes you . . . rush into things without –'

'I don't need you to keep me safe,' Anna interrupted. 'You have your Billy-Boy Way of doing things, but I've got my way, too. I know I can jump in head first, but we're all in this together, and I can help!'

'Listen,' Jimmy said. 'I know you've both got things to talk about, but there's no time now. Anna, we need to tell you what we've found out. This is HUGE!' Quickly he explained to Anna what they'd seen and heard.

'No way!' Anna said when he'd finished. 'Scary Red has stolen *hundreds* of children?'

'And she's about to steal another one, she's going to –' Billy said.

They heard the sound of snuffling and boots on grass.

'Shhh! She's coming!' Jimmy whispered. The three of them scrambled into the nearby trees.

'You might not do things the same way, but jumping in head first is what Anna does best,' Jimmy said. 'You can't stop Anna from being herself and she won't let herself get caught. I know she won't.'

Billy sighed. 'Looking after each other is what friends do,' he said. 'I'd do the same for all of you.'

'I know,' said Jimmy. 'But friends also trust each other and accept that everyone has different ways of doing things. Anna acts first and thinks later, but she's also clever and quick. She cares about people. And that's why she jumped through the window – she couldn't stand the idea of another child being stolen and not doing something about it.'

'I suppose so,' said Billy. 'And at least she has the flint. Hopefully we can use it like a long-distance walkie-talkie.'

'See, that's what *you* do – solve problems the Billy-Boy Way, finding solutions that none of us would have thought of. Me? I do the nature thing – and I'm incredibly wise, of course.' Jimmy winked at Billy. 'Then Andy's got the weapon!'

'*Incredibly wise?*' Billy said with a smile. 'Not

sure about that, Jimmy.'

'Oi! We're all different and that's what makes us magic,' Jimmy said. 'And together, we make the best team.'

Billy smiled again.

'Actually, if you think about what Anna's just done, she's the bravest person we know,' Billy said with pride. '*Go on*, Anna, wherever you are. You've got this.'

'You're right,' Jimmy said. 'Anna is the best, and right now, there's nothing we can do to help her. But let's hope we *can* help Andy and whoever else is in that basement with him. Let's go!'

'No way!' cried Autumn and Jesse in unison, wide-eyed. 'Did all that really happen, Dad?'

A big red double-decker bus boomed past the bedroom window, and a few cars beeped outside.

'I can't believe Scary Red stole all of those children,' Jesse said. 'I don't like her, I really don't like her, *at all*.'

'And never eating!' Autumn said. 'How boring. Imagine never having the excitement of making delicious S'mores with oozy, sticky melted marshmallows and chewy biscuits.' She licked her lips, thinking about the sweet treats.

'Or lovely little tacos with zingy salsa!' said Jesse, getting into the food chat. 'Oh, and those fluffy little bao buns with crispy pork and barbecue sauce inside that we had last week.'

'No wonder she's so awful and mean. I would be, too, if I hadn't eaten for over a hundred years!' Autumn said. 'But, Dad, it all seems pretty bad?

Does this story have a happy ending?'

'Well, Anna, your mum, is on the case with Scary Red, so what do you think?' I asked.

'You and Mum were bickering even when you were our age!' Jesse said with a cheeky grin. 'Some things haven't changed.'

'We don't bicker,' I said.

'You do!' they yelled, in unison again, and started reeling off all the examples they could think of.

'You tell her off for putting tomatoes and chocolate in the fridge.'

'Rightly so,' I replied.

'You squeeze the toothpaste from the top, and she squeezes it from the bottom.'

'She always snoozes her alarm and wakes you up.'

'You don't load the dishwasher in the right way.'

'Mum cleans around you while you're cooking.'

'Oh! And Mum uses that big, round spoon to eat

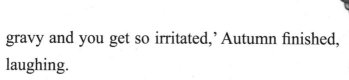

gravy and you get so irritated,' Autumn finished, laughing.

'I mean, who uses a soup spoon with a roast dinner?' I argued, but I couldn't help but laugh with them. Thoughts of Scary Red were forgotten for the night.

'Well, maybe bickering was the start of true love,' said Autumn with a smile.

'That's a long way off in our story yet,' I told her. 'And I think maybe our story is on pause for now, too. Time for sleep!'

The next night, the kids were ready for bed early, so we could continue with our adventures in Waterfall Woods.

I'd started telling my story to help Autumn see that even though she had a hard time with reading and school, she would find her own way through things – just like I'd done. But now, as I

remembered more and more about my Waterfall
Woods adventures, I was also loving getting to
share some of my childhood with Autumn and
Jesse – showing them that I wasn't just boring
old Dad!

That night, Anna had joined us to listen to the
next part of the story. She, too, liked the fact that
the kids were starting to think that their parents
might just be awesome after all.

'Right, ready?' I asked the twins. 'We've still got
a long way to go . . .'

Autumn took a deep breath. 'Yes! You've got to
tell us where Mum went with Scary Red. And what
happened to all those police in the village looking
for Wilfred? Did Bilfred ever get out of his walled
garden? And what about the other Giants? And
you've still not told us how you got your scar! You
know, the one that goes right across your chest.'

As she paused, I jumped in. 'Whoa, slow down,
darling! Let's get back to where we left off last
night and we'll start to find the answers . . .'

Chapter 9

Andy's Rescue

While Anna was off with Scary Red, Billy and Jimmy were cracking on with their own mission: saving Andy!

'ANDYYYYYYY!' Billy yelled as they walked back into the house.

'Billy! Keep it down,' said Jimmy. 'Scary Red might be gone, but we don't know where her Rangers are.'

'She sent them all off, Jimmy, stop worrying,' Billy replied. 'Maybe now's the time to be like Anna and just get stuck in.'

And then . . .

'Billyyyyyyy. Is that youuuuuuu?' a muffled voice shouted.

They looked at each other. That voice was unmistakable. It was Andy! They raced out of the room.

'Andy! Where are you?' cried Billy.

'In the basement!' came Andy's reply. 'We're locked in!'

'Just keep shouting, and we'll follow your voice!' Jimmy cried back.

'I thought we had to be quiet?' Billy said with a raised eyebrow.

'Well, the quicker we find him, the quicker we can get out of here,' Jimmy said. 'Come on, I've had enough of this place.'

They followed Andy's cries and ran down a staircase that led to the basement. At the bottom of the stairs was another corridor, and as they made their way along it, Andy's voice rang out from behind one of the doors.

'Andy!' Billy cried. 'We're here! We've come to rescue you!'

'I knew you'd find us,' came Andy's voice from the other side of the door.

'Scary Red said she'd kidnapped someone else.

Who's with you?' Jimmy asked.

'You're not going to believe this . . . it's Bruno,' replied Andy.

'Hi, Billy! Hi, Jimmy!' Bruno's voice sounded sheepish.

'Bruno!' Billy said. 'What are *you* doing here?'

'He followed me into the woods and got caught by those robots – he was already here when Scary Red brought me back,' Andy explained. 'Bruno says he's hungry, though. Got any snacks?' Even Billy and Jimmy could hear the sound of his gurgling tummy.

Billy reached into his backpack to find his emergency biscuit stash, pushing a handful of squished Garibaldis under the tiny space beneath the door.

The sound of crunching was soon heard. 'I knew we could count on you for emergency snacks, Billy Boy,' Andy said.

'Right, we need to get you out of here,' said Billy.

He and Jimmy searched the door for any kind of lock or opening system. But there was nothing.

'How did she lock you in?' asked Jimmy.

'The doors just closed automatically,' said Andy. 'I managed to get them open by triggering the smoke alarms, but they caught us again and now they're locked firmly.'

Jimmy ran his hands over the walls and around the door, looking for any kind of secret button or opening, when suddenly he felt a vibration and heard . . .

SHWOOW!

A block the size of a Rubik's cube glided out from the wall.

'Whoa, what is this?' Jimmy picked it up carefully. And as he

did so, a projection of a diagram
showing the layout of the house
popped out from the box.

'Chi-a-r . . .' Billy
said, trying to sound out
the words next to the
image. 'What does it say?'

'"Chiaroscuro system",' Jimmy told him.
'But I don't know what that means.'

Billy waved his hand through the projection in
awe. The movement caused the diagram to change,
expanding to show a 3D rotating image of the
building. Billy might have struggled with words, but
making sense of images or models was something he
found easy. He did it all the time with his gadgets
and inventions – to him it was just a different way of
communicating. Instinctively he moved his hand
around the model, making it spin, pinching his
fingers to zoom in and out. This was unlike anything
he'd ever seen before – like something from the
future – yet somehow Billy found himself knowing
exactly what to do.

'Jimmy, look, I think this could be the answer,' he said. 'Give us a second, Andy and Bruno, we're working on it!'

Billy pinched and pulled his fingers, navigating around every room of the house. All sorts of symbols popped up as he moved through the images and Billy guessed they had to be controls for different parts of the building – temperature, lights, windows, doors. If he found the basement, maybe, just maybe, he could use it to get Andy and Bruno out.

He moved through the diagram and into the virtual basement, trying the first symbol he came across. The lights flickered out and they were plunged into darkness apart from the glowing diagram in the air.

'Hey!' shouted Andy.

'Who turned out the lights!' Bruno whimpered.

Billy quickly hit the symbol again and the lights came back on.

'What about those squares?' Jimmy suggested, pointing at a dark square next to an empty square outline. Billy pressed on it.

Some words appeared in the air.

'"Restricted area",' Jimmy read out. '"Continue?"'
Billy tapped on the word and crossed his fingers. The
door in front of them whooshed open. They were
greeted by Andy and Bruno, both with huge smiles of
relief on their faces.

Billy stuffed the white cube into his backpack, the
diagram of the house immediately vanishing from the
air. 'I reckon this might come in handy,' he said.

'Well done, guys!' Andy beamed, giving both his

friends the biggest hug.

'Yeah, thanks, I suppose,' Bruno mumbled. Billy rolled his eyes – even when they had rescued him from a life-or-death situation, Bruno couldn't be nice to them.

'Right, we need to get out of here,' Jimmy said.

Andy, Jimmy and Bruno ran out of the basement and headed for the stairs. Billy went to follow, but found his attention drawn to a room just a short way along the corridor. The door was open and there was a blue glow coming from inside, as well as a low humming noise. He hadn't noticed it before in their determination to rescue Andy and Bruno.

'Come on, Billy, what are you waiting for?' Andy called back to him.

'I just want to see what's in here . . .' Billy said. He peered into the room – it was almost completely empty except for a plinth in the middle with a clear box on top.

'Hey!' Billy shouted to the others. 'Come here!'

'Billy, come on, we've got to go!' Jimmy said, as the other boys walked into the room. But even he was fascinated by what he saw.

A blue stone the size of a tennis ball sat inside the clear box. It was emitting an incredible light, bathing the room in blue – they could almost feel it hum. Two gold wires ran from the bottom of the stone into a bigger cluster of wires, which ran down the length of the plinth, before scattering in all directions, running like tree roots under the clear glass floor.

'This must be anthisalite, too,' Jimmy said, his eyes fixed on the blue glow. 'It looks just like the stones in our buzzpacks.'

'And I think those wires mean it's powering the whole house,' Billy said in amazement.

Andy and Bruno had moved to look at a glass case on the other side of the room. It contained blue stones of varying sizes, from big to small, each with a symbol next to it.

'Guys, look at these – what do these icons mean?' Andy wondered aloud, a blue glow illuminating his face. 'I can't work it out.'

'This one looks like our buzzpacks,' said Billy, coming over. 'And this one is like Scary Red's

shoes . . . I think these are batteries.'

'I don't think it's good news that she has this much anthisalite,' Jimmy said. 'Remember what Chief Mirren said about its power, Billy? It shouldn't be out of the volcano like this.'

'So these stones hold power?' Andy said with amazement. 'Wow, imagine if we had this back home in our world, instead of burning wood and oil.'

Jimmy's eyes widened. 'It would be epic!' His face fell. 'But people would want to dig up every last piece, which would destroy this beautiful world and all the creatures here.'

'You're right, Jimmy. So no one can know,' Billy agreed. 'Twinky promise, everyone?' he asked, and they all linked little fingers, even Bruno.

'I have no idea what's going on or what you're talking about,' Bruno admitted, 'but fine, I promise.'

'Right, I think we definitely need to report back to the Sprites,' said Jimmy, walking out of the room.

Andy and Bruno followed, leaving Billy alone. He stared at the case of stones, almost hypnotized by the blue glow. Carefully he plucked a small stone the size of a marble from the case and stuffed it into his backpack before rushing from the room to join the others.

'Now, let's get out of here,' he said, and all the boys shot up the staircase, back into the entrance hall. They were just about to run out of the front door, when . . .

'Stop immediately, and hold your hands up!' a robotic voice demanded.

173

They spun round to see a Ranger hovering in the living room, its weapon pointed towards them.

'SCATTER!' Billy shouted, thinking quickly.

The kids dispersed, but the Ranger had locked on to Billy. Wherever he went the Ranger followed, and before he knew it he'd been captured and pinned to the floor, so he couldn't move. Then a hatch opened at the base of the Ranger's neck and out came a little miniature arm with two sharp prongs, electricity buzzing between them.

Just when Billy thought it was the end for him, out of nowhere a familiar shadow came clomping along. It was Bruno. He selflessly dived on top of the Ranger and tried to wrestle it off. In the commotion, the robot let go of Billy and now had Bruno pinned to the floor, the same weapon poised in front of his fearful face, ready to electrocute him.

All of a sudden the lights from the Ranger's face went out and it fell, motionless, to the side of Bruno.

'Wha-what happened?' Bruno said.

Andy's little face popped out from behind the Ranger and said, 'I turned it off – there's a button on the back.' Pride glowed from his face. 'I thought it might be like my toys at home: hold it down for three seconds and it shuts down. And it worked!'

'Wow,' Jimmy said. 'Well done, Andy.'

'Well, it's actually a system reboot, which in theory means we can reprogram it to work for us, but I wouldn't know how to do it . . .' Andy continued.

'Whatever, you're a genius,' said Billy, and went round giving Andy and Jimmy a high five.

Then he reached Bruno . . . 'Bruno, I know we've had our differences in the past, but I really appreciate you stepping in to save my life just then. I've never been more relieved to see your Dr. Marten boots!' Billy said, chuckling.

'It was a bit weird, wasn't it?! But to be honest I didn't think at all – I just did it!' said Bruno. The boys high-fived.

'There's nothing like a robot battle in a magical world to end a rivalry, eh?!' Andy said.

'Right, how do we get back to Balthazar from here?' Billy asked.

'Let's look at the map,' Jimmy said, taking the

white cube out of Billy's bag. A detailed map of the house pinged up in the air in front of them once more.

'Wait, look,' Andy said, pointing at a white blinking dot. 'I think that's the Ranger we've just turned off. It's in the right place in the house.'

'You're right, Andy!' said Jimmy. 'And that means we can use this to show us where the other Rangers are . . .'

Billy pinched the map again to zoom out further, and they all watched as more dots showed up. Some were in the air, some in the woods, but a lot looked like they were in a huge network of walled gardens.

Jimmy tapped on one of the robot dots and up popped an identity card – among other things, it said 'Directive: Collect Walled Garden 25 produce'.

'They must each have a job to do,' Jimmy said. 'Hey, Billy, does this map match up to the one the Sprites had?'

Back when they had first discovered Balthazar, they'd also been shown an old map by the Sprites. It had some pieces missing, one of which Bilfred had, but they were still hoping to find more. Billy rummaged around in his backpack and pulled out the unfinished map. He held it up to the image: it was a near-perfect fit.

'Guys, I think we've also found out where Terra Nova is,' Jimmy said slowly. He pointed to what looked like a huge glowing city.

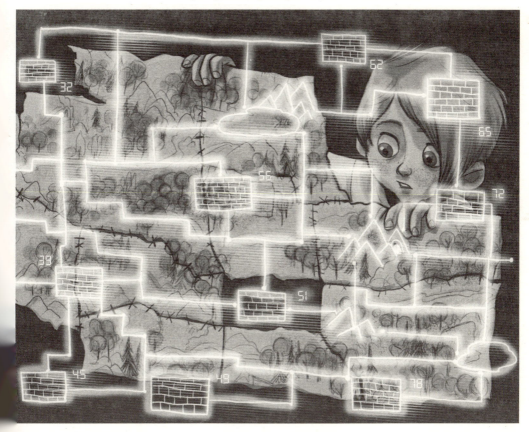

There was silence as the boys were in awe of the sheer magnitude of the world they were getting involved with. 'I think at least it should be easy to shut down the Rangers with this,' suggested Jimmy.

Billy shook his head and said, 'We don't want Terra Nova to suspect anything – growers gotta keep growing, and Rangers gotta keep ranging. Let's try rebooting them, like Andy said earlier. Then perhaps we can get them to work for us instead.'

'Let me have a look,' said Jimmy, searching for the Rangers setting. 'YES! I think I can reprogram them to recognize us as friends, not foes – I just need to scan our faces.' And, with that, all the boys lined up in front of the hologram, where a light danced over their faces.

'What about Anna?' Billy asked.

Jimmy paused. 'Haven't you got a photo of her?'

'No!' Billy answered.

'Come on, Billy, I've seen it.'

Billy blushed, rummaged in his backpack and pulled out a picture of Anna. Jimmy smiled and held it up in front of the cube.

'Right, the Rangers now think we're in command,'
said Jimmy.

'So that's one problem sorted . . .' said Billy.

Just at that moment, something silver flitted by
and sat on Billy's shoulder.

'Finally! It's taken me ages to find yous lot!' said
Basil, out of breath.

'Basil!' Billy said, happy to be reunited with his
Sprite friend. 'Did you get Wilfred to Bilfred's garden?'

'Yes, I took Mr Revel and then wents back to
Balthazar as quickly as I could. When I got there,
Chief Mirren told me that Anna had run off, so –
thinking that she must have heard Cassia and
Rosemary tell the chief directions to where yous was –
I saids I would come and make sure yous weres all
OK,' Basil said.

'Anna did come here,' Jimmy told the little Sprite.
'But now she's gone. She followed Scary Red into a
window in the air!'

'A windows in the air? I think yous got a lot to
catch me up on!' Basil said.

'Um, excuse me . . . Wh-wh-what on earth are
you?' Bruno interrupted, stammering in total
confusion.

Basil, now used to humans being surprised when
they first met him, simply replied: 'I's a Sprite.
Mythical, not magical. And you might not know me,
but I knows you very well.'

'Do you?' Bruno said, surprised.

'Yes. Last time I saw yous, you were very naughty,

and I had to teach you and your friends a bit of a lesson. You were wearing pants with "Wednesday" on 'em – and even I knew it was a Friday! Three days? Yous be disgustin'! But it looks likes, Bruno, you has gone from the dark side to the Sprite side?' he said with a kick and a spin in the air.

Bruno looked sheepish.

'He hasn't said sorry yet, but he has tried to save my life – and actions speak louder than words!' Billy admitted.

'That's the spirit,' said Basil with a grin.

'Basil,' said Billy, 'I threw the flint necklace to Anna before she followed Scary Red. Does it work no matter how far away you are from each other?'

'I woulds thinks so,' replied Basil. 'I managed to sends a message from our magical world to yours, didn't I? Heres, use mine to check on Anna,' he said, handing Billy his necklace.

As the others eagerly told Basil everything they'd discovered, Billy rubbed Basil's flint while thinking of the message he wanted to send to Anna:

ANNA! ARE YOU OK? BILLY.

After a couple of nail-biting minutes, a message returned:

I'M FINE. SO FAR, SCARY RED HAS FAILED.

The boys then asked, **WHERE ARE YOU?**

And she replied:

NOT SURE WHERE I AM. IT'S HOT.

Then, a moment later:

GOT TO GO. SCARY RED ON THE MOVE!

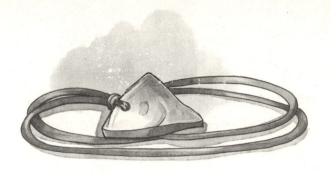

Chapter 10

To Steal a Child

As soon as she had stepped through the window, Anna was hit by a hot, perfumed heat. She quickly clambered up into the nearest tree to get out of sight of Scary Red and Cutter and to get a better view of her surroundings.

The sun was high in the sky, causing the red-coloured mountains in the distance to glow. The sounds from the birds were completely different to anything Anna had ever heard – the furthest she'd been before today was the Isle of Wight, and there certainly wasn't unusual-sounding wildlife there.

They had emerged on a street that was lined with bungalows that all looked the same, each with its own uniform front garden and porch. Anna could see lots of people cooking on their barbecues, sitting in the shade, and chatting and laughing. As their voices reached her in the tree, Anna recognized the accent – they all sounded like the characters in her favourite TV show, *Neighbours*, so she had to be in Australia!

Scary Red and Cutter were strutting down the middle of the street, the dog's noses twitching at the irresistible smell of the cooking sausages. As they walked away, Anna lowered herself quietly to the ground and started to follow at a safe distance.

Just a few houses down, Scary Red pulled into the shadows at the side of a bungalow, where she tapped her bracelet and a map appeared, suspended in the air in front of her. Anna gasped in awe – she'd never seen anything like it before!

'Take me to the Borolama community,' Scary Red said, and a dotted line showing directions appeared on the image. 'Remember Grower 57, Cutter? She was good, wasn't she? She came from here, too. First Nations children seem to be more connected with nature – so their gardens produce not just quantity, but quality. Just what I need.'

She tapped her bracelet to close the map and strode out of the shadows with Cutter, heading up the suburban street. Anna followed in hot pursuit.

A short while later, she stopped in front of a community centre. It was a simple single-storey structure, with a corrugated iron roof – it might not have looked much, but the riot of colour coming from the planters and pots that billowed out from the space around it set it apart, as well as the chattering and laughter that came from the crowd of people inside.

Scary Red walked Cutter behind a bush, hiding him out of sight, then she went confidently straight into the building.

COMI
CE

Anna didn't know what to do, she was utterly torn! Part of her just wanted to scream out and tell everyone that this was an evil woman who wanted to snatch children. But she thought about what Billy had said about her jumping in without thinking.

She was just a kid and a stranger here, so why would they trust her? She might make things worse or get into trouble. And if Scary Red realized she'd been followed, what would stop her leaving and then Anna could end up stuck in Australia with no way home! No, she had to be careful and just stay close, and do whatever she could to stop Scary Red from taking a child back through the tear.

Quickly, she grabbed the flint necklace and sent Billy a message:

I CAN'T FIGHT SCARY RED ALONE HERE. TOO RISKY. WILL TRY TO GET HER BACK THROUGH THE WINDOW. BE READY! I'LL TAKE ON RED – YOU SORT THE DOG.

WE'LL BE WAITING, came the reply, **LET US KNOW WHEN YOU'RE CLOSE!**

Anna put the necklace back under her T-shirt and

scuttled around to the back of the community centre, weaving in and out of massive pots. She spotted Scary Red through a window: she was talking to a woman in a floral dress. Anna crept closer, hoping to eavesdrop to find out what was happening inside.

'I work for a charity called Green Shoots.' Scary Red's voice floated out through the window. 'We donate funds to community projects that get kids into growing, sharing the love of nature.'

Her Australian accent sounded perfect to Anna; the other woman would have no idea she was lying. She even sounded friendly!

'Well, we could definitely do with some help,' the lady replied. 'Everything you see here has been donated and gifted. We do our best to help and inspire local kids, but I can't tell you how much any money would make a difference here.'

'It's not easy to keep this place going,' another voice added. 'And our community really needs us – this is a safe place for children when parents are working, helping to keep them happy, laughing and well fed.'

'We also share the values and culture of the indigenous ancestors, making it relevant to modern life,' the first lady said.

'Well, that sounds like just what we're looking for at Green Shoots,' said Scary Red. 'We have lots of cash just waiting for a worthy project like yours. I would love to speak to one of your children to see what it is they think they need. Is there anyone who is really good at growing?'

'Ah, that would be Ruby – she's a little gem,' the second lady said. 'We call her the Green Queen. She could grow a veg patch on a speck of dust, that kid.'

'Perfect. Could I speak with Ruby, then we'll do some paperwork to start the funding process?'

'Well, I suppose that would be OK,' the first lady said, sounding a little unsure. Anna's heart leapt. Maybe they wouldn't let Scary Red speak to Ruby?

'If it's inconvenient, I could come back. Although, I am seeing lots of other projects today so I can't guarantee the funding will still be available,' Scary Red pushed.

'No, it's fine,' the first lady said quickly. 'Ruby is

just outside, why don't we go and see her in action.'

Anna waited a few moments and then risked peeking through the window. The ladies had gone. Anna scurried around to the front of the building, and spotted Scary Red being introduced to a small girl who was sitting at a table outside, next to a door that led back into the centre.

'Now, Ruby,' the first woman began. 'This lovely lady from a charity wants to ask you some questions.' She sat down next to Ruby.

'Actually, could I trouble you for a glass of water?' Scary Red asked.

'Of course. Nancy, could you please go inside and get some water for our guest?' The second lady nodded and went into the building to get the drink.

Anna realized with horror what Scary Red was doing. *She's trying to get rid of the adults*, Anna thought. *She wants Ruby alone!*

Scary Red sat down and subtly angled herself towards the door. Then, she flicked her wrist under the table and instantly there was the sound of a glass smashing and liquid spilling, followed by a cry.

'Excuse me a minute,' the first lady said. 'I'd better go and help!'

Scary Red wasted no time and turned to the small girl. 'Hello, Ruby. I just need to ask you a few questions. It won't take long.'

'Sure,' said Ruby.

'Do you know this flower?' Scary Red asked,

opening up a little box. 'This won a prize for the sweetest-smelling flower, it's really very special.'

'Oh, I've never seen a flower like that before,' Ruby said, leaning closer. 'And I love flowers and plants!'

'Well, go ahead and smell it. You're going to love it. Have a really long sniff because the scent changes . . .'

Ruby did as she was told, and after just one whiff her eyes became heavy and she soon slumped on the table, fast asleep. In one swift move, Scary Red swooped Ruby up and strode off, whistling for Cutter, who appeared from his hiding place. The community centre was so busy, no one noticed as she walked away.

Anna knew Scary Red would waste no time getting back to the woods, so she quickly sent a message on the flint.

SCARY RED HAS GOT SOMEONE! SHE'S COMING! BE READY!

Message sent, she raced after her, and as they arrived at the same suburban street they'd started from, she watched as once again Scary Red closed her eyes, spun the stone on her staff and opened up a new tear. Anna willed her to put down Ruby – that way she could try to keep the girl here while she somehow bundled both herself and Scary Red through the window. But it seemed Scary Red wasn't taking any chances, and she kept hold of Ruby in one hand while wafting the window open with her other.

As it started to open, Anna could see the incredible, shimmering view of the magical wood and Scary Red's extraordinary house.

She held her breath, hoping the boys were ready and waiting, and that together they could stop Scary Red and somehow get Ruby back home safely . . .

Chapter 11

To Save a Child

In the clearing by Scary Red's house, Billy, Jimmy, Andy, Bruno and Basil stood in a line on high alert, their backs to the house, waiting for the window to appear so they could spring into action.

They didn't have to wait long. A shimmering silver line appeared in front of them, getting bigger and bigger until the world beyond started to come into view through the slice in the air. And there, on the other side, was a fierce-looking Scary Red, holding a sleeping girl in her arms.

Billy strained his eyes, hoping to get a glimpse of Anna, but she was nowhere to be seen. His heart started to race: what if the window closed before she could come through? Or what if Scary Red had realized she was being followed and hurt Anna? As his panic grew, Billy forced himself to take a deep breath – he just had to trust that Anna knew what she was doing. For now he needed to focus on stopping Scary Red. That's what Anna would want. That's why she put herself in danger.

Scary Red stepped out of the window and into the clearing, completely oblivious to the welcome committee waiting for her. Cutter followed closely behind.

'ARGGGHHH!' Much to the surprise of the others, Bruno yelled and charged forward. Little did they know that Bruno actually had a plan. As soon as he'd heard Scary Red had a hound that needed distracting, he thought of his next-door neighbour's dog that he tried to avoid at all costs. He'd devised a clever way of running and jumping on low-hanging branches, so he could stay out of harm's way. It wasn't foolproof, but he hoped it was enough to provide a distraction. He ran, arms waving, towards Cutter before veering off into the woods as the dog gave chase.

'What's going on?' Scary Red cried, utterly bewildered.

'We're here to stop you stealing another child!'
Jimmy shouted.

'That's right,' Basil added. 'Wes know whats yous
been up to!'

A sudden blur of movement came from behind
Scary Red, and she spun round in surprise.

'Where did you come from?' she bellowed, now face
to face with a furious-looking Anna. 'What do you think
you are doing?!'

'It's like my friends said. We're stopping you and
saving Ruby!' Anna replied.

Billy grinned with relief. Anna was OK, and she was back where she belonged!

The woman shrieked in frustration and dropped the sleeping Ruby. Jimmy quickly stepped in to pull her to safety. 'Silly children. I've been doing this for YEARS! How do you think *you're* going to stop *me*? It's time someone taught you all some manners.'

She raised her staff and pointed it straight at Anna. 'I think I'll start with you, *young lady*. It seems like you need to learn how to be ladylike!' Her face

twisted and scrunched into an evil expression as the stone on her staff started to glow. She lunged forward, but, acting quickly, Anna rolled out of the way, easily missing the lightning bolt shooting out of the staff. Scary Red screeched and fired a second bolt. Again, Anna dodged it by jumping up into the closest tree, well out of reach.

Billy grabbed a handful of stones and hurled them at Scary Red, trying to stop her from hurting Anna.

'Leave her alone!' he cried.

The woman spun round and pointed her staff directly at Billy. 'Fine. Seeing as you're so protective of your little friend, perhaps I'll start with you instead!' she cried, cackling. 'But I don't like the feel of you – you're too . . . good! Disgusting!'

'No!' Anna shouted. She jumped from the tree and ran towards Billy, trying to get between him and the staff. But she was too late. A flash came from the stone and hit Billy, creating a deep slash that went right across his torso. Crying out, he fell to the floor.

'Billy!' Jimmy ran to his best friend's side.

Anna looked at Scary Red with fury. As she did, she spotted Andy, who had used the drama to sneak behind Scary Red and was now on all fours between her and the closing window. He looked at Anna and motioned his head, silently communicating his plan to her.

The window had already started to close, so, knowing there were only seconds left, Anna ran forward with a cry and, using all of her might, jumped and kicked Scary Red in the stomach. Stunned, the woman flew backwards, tumbled over Andy and fell through the window, dropping her staff as she went.

They were just in time. The window in the air closed, trapping Scary Red on the other side of the world in an instant. They'd done it! Scary Red was gone, and Ruby was safe, but as Anna turned back to Billy and Jimmy it was obvious there'd been a price to pay. Billy was seriously hurt.

Anna ran over to her friend. 'Are you OK?' she asked, sitting behind Billy, so he could rest his head on her lap.

'I think that staff cut me pretty deeply,' Billy replied, wincing.

Bruno ran back into the clearing, panting with exhaustion and sopping wet. 'Billy!' he cried. 'What happened to you?'

'Scary Red got him with her staff,' Andy explained. 'What about you? What happened to the dog, and why are you soaking wet?'

'I jumped in the river to try to get rid of that awful thing,' Bruno said. 'I couldn't think of what else to do! But it didn't work, the dog followed me in. We got swept downstream and I managed to grab hold of an overhanging branch just before a waterfall. The dog fell over the edge. Boom, gone.'

'You're a hero, Bruno,' Jimmy said. 'An absolute hero. Saving the day . . . twice!'

'Thanks,' Bruno replied, his cheeks turning slightly pink. He wasn't used to compliments, but he was starting to like how it made him feel to have friends who weren't just hanging around because they were afraid of him.

Billy let out a groan from the ground.

'I can help yous, Billy,' Basil said, flying to sit by his friend. 'Us Sprites uses remedies from nature. I'll gather some herbs and perhaps yous all can help me bash them together into a poultice.'

'A what?' asked Andy.

'A poultice is like a natural plaster,' explained Jimmy. 'It stops things from getting infected.'

'We needs calendula and yarrow. That'll helps to keep infections at bay. There should be some around here if we look.' He flitted away into the woods to start the search.

'Come on, Andy, Bruno, let's help him,' said Jimmy,

and the three of them followed the Sprite into the trees.

'I'm so sorry I was cross with you,' Anna whispered to Billy. 'It was silly of us to fight. But I'm here now and you're going to be OK.'

'I'm sorry, too,' Billy muttered. 'Anna, I'm so tired.'

'You should sleep. We'll look after you.' She pushed his floppy hair out of his eyes, trying not to look too closely at the bleeding wound on his chest. Billy mumbled in response, drifting off to sleep.

It was only then, as the clearing fell silent, that Anna noticed the quiet sobs of Ruby. Whatever spell Scary Red had cast on the girl had worn off, and she was crouched down next to a tree, looking round in fear. Anna gently moved the sleeping Billy from her lap and walked over to the girl.

'Hi, Ruby. My name's Anna,' she said, in a comforting tone. 'I know this is really weird, but don't worry, you're safe with me and my friends – we won't hurt you.'

The girl looked at Anna, her face damp with tears. 'I don't know what happened. One minute I was at the

centre, the next I'm here with you. Where am I?
What's going on?'

'Well . . .' Anna paused, not quite sure how to
explain to Ruby that she was in a whole different
country on the other side of the world! 'You are quite
far away from Australia now. You're in England.'

Ruby's mouth fell open. 'England? But how?'

'It's not easy to explain, but remember that woman
who you were speaking to? Well, she's somehow able
to open windows to different places and she brought

you here. She's not . . . a good person, so we stopped her. Now we just have to work out how to get you back home.'

Ruby seemed stunned into silence, but Anna was relieved that she had at least stopped crying. 'Why don't you tell me a little about yourself?' Anna asked gently, trying to keep the young girl talking.

'I'm eight and a half years old, and I'm from Mparntwe – that's Alice Springs – in Australia. I live with my foster family there,' she said, starting to cry again. 'Oh no, they'll be worried when they realize I'm missing!'

'I've been fostered before, so that's something we have in common,' said Anna. 'And don't worry, we will get you home. Me and my friends have been getting out of some serious scrapes recently, so you're in good hands. We just need to work out how to use this thing.' Anna picked up the staff that Red had dropped and twirled it round in her hand. The stone at the top gleamed as it caught the last of the sunlight.

'Is he all right?' Ruby asked, pointing towards Billy.

'He's not great,' Anna said. 'But he'll be OK. He has to be.'

At that moment the boys and Basil returned from their search.

'We found them!' Jimmy cried to Anna. They all rushed towards Billy.

'Nows we just need to bash them up to get the good juices,' instructed Basil. And Jimmy and Andy immediately got to work pounding the herbs between two rocks. As liquid started to appear, Basil scooped the herbs up and pressed them on to Billy's wound. Billy groaned in his sleep.

'That should keep him comfortable, for now,' said Basil.

'What is THAT?' Ruby asked suddenly, pointing at Basil.

'I is not a THAT!' Basil replied with a huff. 'I is a Sprite.'

'You're so small!' Ruby said in amazement.

'Well, look who's talking,' he said, and she laughed. He flew around the little girl, playing with her hair, tickling her ears and making her giggle.

'There isn't just Basil,' Anna told Ruby. 'There's a whole community of Sprites here in these woods.'

'No way! Where do you live?' Ruby asked.

'Balthazar. It's beautiful – we've got a castle, rainbow waterfalls, juicy fruits and veggies! Our ancestors used to live there with Giants, and we've just returned.'

'Giants?' Ruby asked, looking worried. Bruno's eyes also widened at the thought.

'Yes, Giants. But don't worry, one of them is our friend. So there's nothing to be afraid of,' said Jimmy. 'I'm Jimmy. And this is Andy and Bruno.'

'I'm Ruby. Wow! This is all so WEIRD! I don't know what I'm doing here at all.'

'Well, if Chief Mirren was here – that's the leader of us Sprites – I think she woulds say that the Rhythm meants for you to be here,' Basil told her.

'The Rhythm?' Ruby asked.

'Whys do I have to keep explaining this to hoomans?' Basil said. 'The Rhythm is life; it's everything. It's balance, harmony, everybody and everythings working together. We're all a part of it, and yous just need to have faith that what yous put in, yous get out.'

'It sounds like Winanga-Li,' Ruby said with a smile. 'It means "hear, listen, know, remember". But my people have lots of ways to say kind of the same thing. It's about harmony and respect for nature.'

'That's the Rhythm,' Basil said with a grin. 'Who are your peoples?' he asked politely.

'My people are First Nation, the indigenous people of Australia,' Ruby said.

'That sounds olds,' Basil mused.

Ruby nodded. 'How old are you?' she asked Basil.

'Never you mind – but Sprites can live for a long time! The oldest Sprite I ever knew was 120 years old!'

'Are you magic?'

'A little bit!'

'What do you eat?'

'Everything – but my favourite is the honey from a binglebong flower,' Basil replied, licking his lips just at the thought of it.

'My favourite is a quandong. A sweet, juicy fruit that my mum and grandma pick.' Tears welled up in Ruby's eyes again as she thought about her family.

'Don't you worry. We'll get you home soon, Ruby,' said Anna reassuringly.

Ruby looked carefully at Anna. She patted her own heart. 'I know you will. I can feel it, right here.'

Billy groaned, pulling everyone's attention back to him.

'He's burning up,' said Jimmy, placing his hand on his friend's head. He looked at Basil. 'What do we do?'

'Let's replace that poultice and get some cabbage leaves on his forehead to cool him down,' said Basil.

'He needs a doctor, but I'm not sure we should move him right now, he's hurting too much,' Anna said.

'Yes, we should stay here a while,' said Jimmy. 'With Scary Red trapped, I think we can risk staying the night here and sleeping in the house.' The friends looked at each other and nodded in agreement. Then Jimmy, Anna, Andy and Bruno carefully lifted Billy from the ground and, with Ruby and Basil at their side, walked inside. They gently placed Billy on the cool marble floor and took care to make sure he was comfortable.

Basil gave everyone some of the leftover berries from their foraging efforts to try to at least get something into their stomachs before bed. Then, finally, they all settled down, putting together a makeshift camp in the giant living room.

A few hours later, Anna woke, her heart racing, as she felt the presence of something strange. She looked up and saw a wisp of beautiful, sparkling white light that danced up and down in a never-ending figure of eight. The wisp then split and turned into two small, illuminated figures standing in front of her. Anna opened her mouth to wake the others, but nothing came out, then for some reason her initial fear quickly turned to calm. She wasn't sure why, but she didn't think these creatures meant them harm.

They glowed softly in the darkness and had soft, sweet features, not quite human, but not unfamiliar either. One of them held their hand out to Anna. Without hesitation she reached forward and as they touched, Anna felt an immediate loving connection.

The second creature waved its hands and Anna gasped as she saw Billy float up into the air, still fast asleep.

Anna was surprised that none of the others stirred, but aside from the creatures the room felt still and frozen, as if everyone else was trapped in time.

The creature holding her hand rose from the floor, bringing Anna with them, until she was floating next to Billy. She watched in wonder as Billy drifted across the room and out of the open window, and then the creature pulled her to follow. Then, in the blink of an eye, Billy and Anna were whooshing through the woods at speed, the glowing creatures alongside them. As they reached the end of the woodlands, they were moving faster and faster. Anna couldn't believe it. Waterfall Woods had surprised her again with its wonder and magic! She looked over at Billy: somehow he was still asleep even as they whizzed through the air.

Eventually they slowed, and Anna and Billy drifted down towards a big redwood tree with the most incredible exposed roots. Anna ducked as they dived in between them and into a tunnel that went under the ground. Ahead of them, the figures' vibrant brightness gently waned in the pure darkness, and then finally they stopped, as Billy was floated gently on to the mossy floor of the cave and Anna landed softly. She knelt down next to Billy.

Anna felt the creature release her hand, and in the darkness of the cave her fear started to rise again.

'Who are you?' she blurted out. 'Where have you taken us? What do you want?'

The cave was bathed in a ghostly glow as the figures gently illuminated the dark again. One of them took Anna's hand once more and said, 'The question is not who are "you" but who are "we". We are the personification of trillions of mycelia. You can call us the Myas.'

Anna realized that the Myas weren't talking out loud, instead it was as if they were speaking directly to her mind. She felt totally hypnotized. Then a flash of recognition sparked Anna's memory. 'Mycelia? Wait, Chief Mirren said you were like mushrooms or something . . . but you don't look like any mushrooms I've ever seen!'

'We are fungi,' they replied. 'But we are more than just mushrooms. We are the extraordinary in the ordinary. The Myas live under the ground and on the ground, we live inside humans and animals. Nothing happens without us, but rarely do we come together in a form like you see before you, unless it's desperately important.'

'Is this because of Scary Red?' Anna asked.

'We will tell you all, but first, we must help your friend.'

The Myas glowed brighter and sank closer to the floor. Anna watched as they got lower until the bottom halves of their bodies were simply part of the floor. Thin tendrils of glimmering light made their way down the glowing bodies, snaking into the mossy carpet. The moss and the light pulsed and grew and stretched towards Billy as he lay on the floor. Anna gasped. What if she was wrong about these creatures? What if they wanted to hurt him?

'Do not be alarmed,' said the Myas. 'We know you are friends of the Rhythm. We will not harm you.'

By now the glowing fibres had completely covered Billy and the light began to pulse with waves of colour. The open wound on Billy's chest started to heal before Anna's eyes as the webs of mycelium went to work, criss-crossing his body, glowing green and blue, until eventually the cut was gone and only a scar remained. The mycelium slowly but surely receded, and Billy took a big breath of air, his eyes flickering open.

'Billy! Are you OK?' Anna dipped down to give him the biggest hug.

'Yes,' he replied, confused. 'I feel great actually. What's going on?'

'It's kind of hard to explain . . .' Anna said.

'We believe you and your friends have the power to change the course of what could be the end of the world as we know it.' The Myas' voices floated into Anna and Billy's minds once again and the children were stunned into silence. 'We are the custodians of both this magical world and yours, helping to support and balance the Rhythm across the realms.

'In your world, we are having to fight many battles to redress the balance, as nature's diversity is being depleted, controlled and hunted. Waterfall Woods on this side of the gate is our safe haven – a place that's unspoiled and in harmony. It gives us the strength to keep going in yours, restoring our power for that fight.

'But now this land is also in danger. We watched you rebalance the Rhythm once before when the damage from your world found its way through our protected gate. So we are asking for your help again.'

'With what?' Anna asked.

'The State known as Terra Nova is taking advantage of the power of nature, taking too much and not putting enough back. You should know that the people of Terra Nova were once from your world, and we mistakenly let them stay. But now, they're working at a rate that is not sustainable. If we do not stop them, they will completely remove harmony from this world and in doing so destroy everything. They think they can outwit the Rhythm itself and go against nature.'

'But what can we do?' Billy said.

'More than you realize. We believe that you and your friends can act now to stop Terra Nova stealing our resources and hurting the Rhythm. We hope you will teach Terra Nova about the Rhythm and therefore about what's right and wrong.'

The web of light began to glow and the presence of the Myas was all around them once more. 'We know it's not going to be easy, but can we rely on you?' The voices echoed in Anna and Billy's heads.

'Yes, we will do it,' Anna said. 'Of course we will.'

'We'll do everything we can,' Billy added.

'Will we ever see you again?' asked Anna.

'It's unlikely you'll see us like *this* again,' they replied. 'But if you want to feel us, then, when you go walking in the woods, get your hands dirty, take your shoes off and stand on the ground. Learn to listen to nature properly. Every human is able to do this if they just allow themselves to tune in.'

And, with that, the Myas took Billy's and Anna's hands, and they retraced their journey back to Scary Red's house. As they whooshed home, the kids could see the glowing mycelium trailing behind, like a little wave. Billy and Anna felt incredibly lucky, if a little scared, that their quirky little gang might just be the key to saving not only this world but their own home, too.

Chapter 12
Mastering the Staff

'Billy, hows are you?' asked Basil, buzzing over Billy's head the next morning.

'I'm . . . really good,' Billy said. He looked down at his chest and the long scar where the wound from the staff had been.

'How have you healed so quickly?' asked Jimmy, staring at Billy's scar.

Billy and Anna exchanged a look. 'Something amazing happened last night,' Billy began. 'But I'm starving! Let's get some breakfast and we'll tell you all about it.'

'Well, I's thinks this calls for a celebration, so I's is goings to make the best breakfast yous ever had in your lives,' Basil said. He took them outside, and, picking up a stick, drew a circle on the ground. 'Billy, Anna, Ruby, you digs out a little pit and build a fire here. Jimmy and Andy, yous go down to the river and find as many round pebbles as yous can.'

'And what about me?' Bruno asked, wanting to be helpful.

'Come on, Bruno, you comes with me. I'll needs some help finding the perfect ingredients,' Basil said, and they went off foraging in the woods.

Soon enough, all the kids and Basil came back to a roaring fire with all the ingredients the Sprite had asked for. 'I even found this big bowl thing in Red's house while looking for things to start the fire with,' Billy said, holding up a white, beautifully crafted marble dish. 'Thought you might need it.'

'That'll be perfect for making my pebble cakes in,' Basil said, and quickly got to work. The kids watched as he tore the flowers of a gividawada plant – which smelt sweet, almost like candy floss – into the bowl. Next, Basil squeezed the centre of an adojo leaf from the top all the way to the bottom, so that teardrops of milk dripped out. Then he took a little Sprite-sized tin out of his pocket and shook in the luminous yellow pollen from the sapphire tree.

'That'll makes the cakes all light, bubbly and fluffy.' Basil explained.

He finished with a vanilla pod even bigger than him, using his little feet to scrape out thousands of incredibly perfumed seeds and pop them into the bowl.

'Right, now, Bruno, I want you to whip up this mixture until it's nice and smooth and shiny.' Bruno did as he was told and started to beat the ingredients with a stick. 'We knows when it's ready by holding up the stick, and when it takes three seconds for the

batter to fall off – just like that – it's perfect. Nows, time for the fun bit . . .'

Basil ordered Andy and Jimmy to place the pebbles they'd found over the fire, until the flames slowly died down.

'Basil, why would you do that?' asked Anna. 'Now we don't have a fire to cook with.'

'I don't wants the flames; I wants the heat. Look, the stones are glowing red. All hot and toasty.'

'Nows, this be the best bit,' Basil continued. 'Bruno, pour that beautiful mixture all over the stones.' Again, Bruno did as he was told, the thick, sweet-smelling cake mix nestling into all the dips and crevices, and within seconds it started to cook on top of all the pebbles. Basil gave Bruno the nod to bring over the pile of multicoloured fruits they'd foraged for earlier. 'Everyone, take a handful and, from a height, scatter,' he instructed. A rainbow of fruit rained down and cooked into the golden batter, the jammy juices rippling out. Basil then stuck seven sticks into the cake, one for each person.

'Billy, penknife, please,' Basil said. Billy handed him

the knife from his backpack and the Sprite sliced between the sticks, creating seven perfect lolli-cakes.

As the kids tucked into the fluffiest, pillowiest, spongiest cakes they'd ever eaten, Billy and Anna told everyone about their late-night adventure.

'Chief Mirren will want to hears all about this,' said Basil when they'd finished. 'I don't think the Myas have ever appeared in this ways before, so things must be bad!'

'Right then, we need to go to Balthazar. Who agrees?' Billy said, and everyone nodded determinedly.

They gathered up their stuff, then Billy went to Scary Red's armoury and came back with buzzpacks for Andy and Bruno. 'I didn't bring one for you, Ruby – I don't think you're quite big enough to wear one of these. But I thought you could hitch a ride with one of us.'

'You can come with me, Ruby!' Anna said with a smile.

They all whooshed upwards, skimming the tops of the trees as they made their way back to the home of the Sprites, Ruby giggling with glee the whole way. Well, almost all of them – Bruno ricocheted like a pinball from tree to tree, but the whoops that were coming from him proved he was loving every minute of it.

As Balthazar came into view, Billy was pleased to see that it was looking much better than when they had left. There were still signs of Scary Red's attack, but the Sprites had done a brilliant job of tidying up in just a short space of time.

Chief Mirren came to greet them. 'You're back! And you've brought some new friends, I see.' She smiled at Ruby and Bruno. 'I'm sure you all have much to tell me. Come inside – I want to hear everything.'

A little while later, they were all gathered around a table inside Balthazar Castle.

'Chief Mirren, do you think you can help me master Scary Red's staff? I want to get Ruby back to Australia as quickly as possible; her family will be worried,' Anna said.

Chief Mirren flew over and peered closely at it. She flitted up and down and round and round, looking at it from all angles to try to understand the strange object.

'It looks to me as if the stone in this staff is a tetrahedron,' she said eventually. 'A perfect crystal prism, in this case made of anthisalite. There are legends about such a stone – two stones, in fact – that allows seamless travel to different places, different times, possibly even different dimensions. As with many other things since you children arrived in our woods, it appears that this legend is in fact the truth.'

'Do your legends say how to use it?' Billy asked.

'They do not, although my instinct would be that, as with much of nature, it's all about intention and belief,' Chief Mirren replied.

Anna's eyes lit up. 'When I watched Scary Red, she always seemed to take a moment, a deep breath, before motioning the staff to make a window. Could that be what she was doing? Focusing on intention?'

Chief Mirren nodded. 'It sounds like it may well have been. But intention is also about clarity and confidence of the mind – see it, feel it, smell it. Picture yourself there, and the world will open up.'

'I'm not very good at just thinking about one thing,' admitted Anna. 'My mum says my mind is always buzzing!'

'You'll need to focus, Anna. I believe you can do it, but the only way to get this working is if you can clear your mind,' Chief Mirren said.

Anna held the staff and closed her eyes. She tried to imagine Alice Springs again. She thought of the warm air, the smell of the barbecues, the laughter of the children at the centre . . .

In front of her, the stone in the staff dropped and began to spin slowly.

Anna's brain whirred as an image of Alice Springs

started to form in her mind, but then she found her attention drifting – she thought of her mum and whether she'd be worried about her, then she thought about poor Bilfred being captured and trapped again in his garden. She heard the argument she'd had with Billy about being left behind, and saw his worried face when she'd jumped into the window to follow Scary Red . . . And, as these thoughts filled her mind, Alice Springs got further and further away.

The spinning stone faltered and started to slow. Ruby let out a small sigh of disappointment and Billy gave her arm a squeeze. 'Don't worry, Ruby,' he said. 'This was just Anna's first try, she never gives up!'

'Go on, Anna,' Jimmy said encouragingly. 'You've got this.'

Anna took another deep breath and tried again. Alice Springs. Warmth. Sausages. Laughter. The Myas asking them to help stop Terra Nova. The Rhythm being in trouble. Billy not thinking she was good enough . . .

Anna opened her eyes. 'I can't do it,' she said.

'When I think about Alice Springs, everything else pops into my mind. It's too much, there are too many things to solve, and I don't know how to do it all.'

'You don't have to do it all,' Billy told her. 'Big problems are just lots of little ones that you can take one at a time. And no one can do *everything*.'

Anna gave him a grateful smile.

'When I want to find calm, and that is quite often,' Andy chipped in, 'I say to myself, "You are the sky, everything else is just weather." It always works for me.'

'I like that,' Anna said, impressed. 'Where did that come from?'

'Back of a cereal packet, I think,' he replied.

'Your friends are right,' said Chief Mirren. 'You're expecting it to come all at once. And you're giving yourself a hard time – don't forget that not all thoughts are true. Those ones that say you can't do it? They're not true. You can do this. Talk to yourself like you're your own best friend. At the end of the day, it's just you versus you – believe in yourself.'

'Anna, I know you're trying your best for me,' Ruby

said, giving her a big hug. 'It's OK. You'll do it!'

'Maybes you should try focusing closer to home?' Basil suggested. 'I can sees and smells Balthazar and our cosy Sprite houses better than anywhere else in the world. So perhaps you need to see if you can get yourself home before trying the other side of the world!'

'You're right, Basil,' Anna said with a nod. 'Home. That's where I should start.'

Anna picked up the staff again and closed her eyes. She thought of home. She imagined her front door, walking in through the small hallway past all the shoes, coats, umbrellas and bags crammed to the side and then up the stairs to her room. She could smell her dad cooking his favourite cottage pie and hear the theme tune to *Dallas* coming from the living room as her mum watched her favourite TV show. She imagined walking into her bedroom, seeing the poster of her favourite band, Duran Duran, on the wall, breathing in the smell of The Body Shop's White Musk perfume . . . She raised the staff and struck the ground with it – just like she had seen Scary Red do.

Billy gasped as he watched the tetrahedron spin faster and faster. It was working, Anna was really doing it!

Slowly, carefully, Anna opened her eyes and stepped forward, her gaze firmly on the spinning crystal.

The prism whirled, picking up even more speed until it was like a mirrored blur with a perfect reflection of itself underneath. Anna let the staff go and again, just as it had with Scary Red, it stayed floating. Anna twisted the pyramid, pulling the top and bottom apart and a tear appeared in the air in front of her.

She pulled at the tear, not allowing her mind to wander from the sights and sounds and smells of her bedroom, and then, there it was. A window into her room. She stepped through, not daring to look at the others in case her attention broke and the tear vanished again.

Staring around in wonder at the fact that she was somehow back in her own bedroom, Anna didn't notice her trainers on the floor and stumbled and fell, causing a loud thump!

'Anna? Is that you up there?' shouted her mum from downstairs. 'Are you OK?'

'Yeah, it's me, Mum,' Anna replied, excitement bubbling in her voice. 'Sorry, I . . . dropped something.'

'I didn't hear you come in, I thought you were still at the holiday club. I hope you and Billy haven't been bickering again?'

'No, Mum, we're fine! I've just . . .' She tried to think of a quick excuse as to why she'd be back home. 'I've come back for a change of clothes; I got muddy. But I'm going back to the club now. We're . . . working on something.'

'OK. Well, be good – and put your dirty clothes in the wash!' her mum yelled back.

Not wanting to push her luck, Anna jumped back through the tear and returned to Balthazar again.

'Anna! You did it!' Billy cried, rushing over to her as she appeared in front of them.

Anna looked shocked. 'Y-yeah, I did! I spoke to my mum!' she replied.

Chief Mirren clapped her little hands together with joy. 'You should be so proud of yourself,' she said. 'OK, shall we try somewhere else? And this time you can practise closing the portal and opening it from the other side. Where is your second-favourite place in the world? Somewhere that's easy to see and feel.'

'Er, Fry Days? The local fish and chip shop. Their food is delicious!' Anna answered, beaming from her successful trip.

'Excuse me,' Bruno piped up, 'I know there's important stuff going on here, but my mum's going to be worried sick. And I'm rather partial to a Fry Days . . .'

'You're right,' Billy said. 'We don't want any more trouble in the village. Anna, do you think you can take Bruno with you? It'll be a test for when Ruby has to go through the window, too.'

Anna nodded. 'I can certainly try. Right, you ready to go home, Bruno? Let's do this.'

'Remember to imagine it fully – see it, smell it, feel it,' reminded Chief Mirren.

Feeling more confident, Anna stood with her eyes

closed and took a deep breath, right into her belly. She imagined the smell of the cooking chips and the sourness of malt vinegar, the sizzle of batter as the fish hit the oil, the rustle of newspaper being wrapped around delicious suppers. Once again the prism spun, and Anna repeated the ritual with the staff, causing a tear in the air that revealed shiny white tables and chairs, an illuminated glass counter topped with bottles of salt, vinegar, pickled eggs and cucumbers, and trays of wooden forks. Then she took Bruno's hand and they confidently stepped through – but this time, as instructed by Chief Mirren, Anna turned and closed the tear behind her. She was just in the nick of time as Mrs Black, the owner, walked in from the back office.

'Hello, Anna, love! Hello, Bruno. Don't normally see you both together. You're a bit early, we're not even open yet. Actually, how did you get in?' Mrs Black said, looking confused.

'Er, the door was on the latch,' Anna lied.

'Well, lucky for you the fryers are up and running, ready for the lunchtime rush. So, Anna, I suppose you want the usual three fish and chips and one scampi and chips?' Mrs Black said, referring to the fact she was rarely seen without Billy, Andy and Jimmy. 'And the usual for you too, Bruno?'

'That would be great,' Anna and Bruno said in unison, their tummies rumbling. 'But we don't have any money,' Anna admitted.

'Don't worry, I'll write you a little IOU. You can pay me back next time,' Mrs Black said with a smile, scribbling on a piece of paper, which she then pinned to the corkboard behind her.

The kids watched as she created five perfect parcels of food, all wrapped up in newspaper. 'Here you go,' Mrs Black said. 'Enjoy! I've even popped some fresh lemon in there for you. And here, have a bottle of Tizer, Anna. I know Billy loves it.'

'Thanks, Mrs Black,' said Anna.

'Yeah, thanks,' replied Bruno, who already had a mouthful of chips.

Mrs Black turned around to wash her hands. 'You're welcome, my love. Now, what do you make of all the police kerfuffle? Where can poor old Mr Revel be, do you think? I was just talking to –' But when Mrs Black turned back, she was surprised to find Bruno stood alone.

'Where'd she go in such a hurry?' Mrs Black asked.

Bruno shrugged, chomping on another couple of chips and hiding a smile.

With her bag of goodies, Anna triumphantly stepped back into Balthazar Castle, an audience clapping wildly at her second success.

'OH MY WORD! Fry Days fish and chips!' Billy said.

'Yum! Perfect salty, vinegary deliciousness,' said Andy.

She settled down on the floor, closely followed by the boys and Ruby, and started to open up the warm parcels. 'I'm starving! Travelling to other places like this really works up an appetite.'

'Basil and Chief Mirren, you're gonna love this,' Jimmy said to the Sprites, who had fluttered down to join the kids.

'Here, let me give you guys a little taster,' said Anna. She tore off two pieces of paper and into each popped a corner of scampi with half a chip, a drip of lemon juice and tiny dollops of tartar sauce and ketchup, then passed them to Chief Mirren and Basil.

'Mmmmm!' said Basil, tucking in. 'This is delicious!'

'It certainly is tasty,' agreed Chief Mirren.

'It's a British classic,' said Billy. 'And it's even better washed down with a little fizzy Tizer.' He poured a capful and passed it to Basil. The Sprite drank it, then immediately burped with such force that it pushed him backwards into Andy's chest.

'Wowzers! Thats is some drinks – I thinks I'll leaves it to you professionals,' Basil giggled.

'What do you think, Ruby?' Andy asked. 'Do you have fish and chips like this back home?'

'Yeah, we have all different types of seafood,' Ruby said, taking a big bite of fish. 'Although it's great that yours are wrapped up in newspaper. That's a cool way to recycle.' She pointed to a headline in the greasy paper.

COMMUNITY IN TEARS AS OLD MAN STILL MISSING

'Oh no,' Billy said. 'I'd forgotten about people being worried about Mr Revel with everything else that's happened since we got to the woods. We need to let the village know that he's OK.'

Anna nodded. 'And now that I've mastered the tetrahedron, I can take Ruby home,' she added. 'They will be worried about her just like everyone is worried about Mr Revel. So we need to get her back. Once we've finished eating, do you want to go home, Ruby?'

Ruby yelped with joy. 'Thank you, thank you!' she said over and over to Anna. 'I can't wait to see my mum and dad.' Then she went quiet.

'What's wrong, little one? Don't be nervous,' said Anna.

'I do really want to go home, but now I'm here, now I've met you, I'm not sure I'm ready to go just yet. It's like you said, Basil, maybe the Rhythm brought me here for a reason? I want to meet your friend Bilfred, as Scary Red took him, too. You kept me safe, but the other children she stole are still here and stuck.'

'Are you sure?' Anna asked.

'Totally sure,' Ruby replied.

Anna nodded approvingly. 'You're a brave Green Queen.'

'Talking of stolen children, maybe this is another job for our friend Jerry Draper?' Billy suggested, thinking of the local reporter who had helped them put a stop to the terrible farm polluting the river and upsetting the Rhythm. 'I think we've got enough information on what Red's been up to to give him another scoop and stop her forever.'

Andy cheered. 'Great idea, Billy!'

'Right. So here's the plan. First we need to take Wilfred back and set things straight in the village – which means going back to Bilfred's garden where Ruby can meet him, too,' Billy said. 'Then we get Jerry on the case to look into the missing kids. Now you guys have set up this holding position – the Rangers and growers are doing what they need to – I reckon we've got two or three days before we're found out.'

'Terra Nova normally contacts Red once a week – I overheard them talking when we were in the house,' Jimmy said. 'Once they try to get hold of her and she's not here, they'll get suspicious pretty fast.'

'Then let's get going!' Andy said.

'Ruby . . . last chance: home, or Bilfred's garden?' Anna asked.

'Bilfred's garden,' Ruby replied confidently.

Chapter 13
Ruby's Gift

Anna stood calmly, eyes closed. It wasn't long before the tetrahedron started to spin and generate its reflection. 'My intention is to go to Bilfred's walled garden, next to his shed,' Anna said. She struck the staff and let it float in the air, then pulled apart the pyramids and the familiar sight of Bilfred's garden appeared.

One by one the kids jumped through, much to Bilfred and Wilfred's shock, surprise and happiness. Even the flowers seemed to be celebrating!

'How'd you do that?' Bilfred asked in amazement.

Billy replied proudly, 'Anna has mastered Scary Red's magical staff – it's like the gate in our tree, but it's mobile.'

'Well, aren't you a clever young lady?' Bilfred said, chuckling.

Bilfred and Wilfred welcomed everyone with cups of tea and open arms. As Bo raced around saying hello to everyone, the kids couldn't help but notice that the garden seemed happier than when they were there last. Flowers were brighter in colour, pollen wafts were more frequent, you could almost hear the plants growing, and there was a contented hum in the air.

Having his brother there had clearly made Bilfred happier than ever, which was reflected in his garden.

'Bilfred, Wilfred, we've got someone to introduce you to as well: this is Ruby, aka the Green Queen – she's from Australia,' said Anna, holding Ruby's hand. Ruby was hiding behind her and looking a little frightened of the rather large Giant.

'Hello, young Ruby. You are very welcome in my garden,' said Bilfred.

'Hi,' said Ruby, looking shy. 'I've never met a Giant before. How did you get so big?'

'I used to be small, just like you. But, when I was a boy, I was brought here,' explained Bilfred. 'I think it's all the good soil and good veg that's made me grow to super size! More soil, more good stuff. More trees, more oxygen – put all that together and everything shoots up.'

'Ruby was stolen by Scary Red, too,' Billy explained. 'We rescued her before Red had a chance to trap her. She wanted to meet you.'

'I love growing things,' Ruby told Bilfred. 'I plant all sorts back home, and it always turns out to be the best fruit and veg in our garden. I love growing tomatoes and capsicums the most.'

'Those are peppers to us,' Jimmy explained.

'But as much as I love growing, I love my family more; I couldn't imagine never seeing them again.' Ruby's face fell. 'I'm sorry that you've been trapped for so long, Bilfred.'

'Don't you worry, little one,' Bilfred said with a smile. 'I was sad for a long time. Even with all the new friends I met in my garden, I still missed my real home. But then Billy, Anna, Andy and Jimmy came and brought my brother back to me.'

'And we're never going to be separated again!' Wilfred added.

'Actually, Mr Revel, about that,' Billy said nervously. 'We think you *do* need to be separated again. Just for a little while. Everyone back home is still really worried about you being missing.'

'Everyone is out looking for you *and* it's all over the local paper,' said Jimmy, holding up the oil-stained piece of newspaper from their fish lunch.

'I didn't think anyone would miss me,' said Wilfred,

sounding surprised. 'I've been all alone in my cottage for as long as I can remember – I guess it's nice to know people do care after all.'

'Wilfred, go back, let them know that you're safe,' Bilfred suggested gently. 'With Scary Red gone, there's no threat to my garden any more and you can come back once you've reassured everyone at home that you're OK.'

'Well, if you think it's a good idea, brother . . .' Wilfred said. 'But I'm not staying for long, just to set things straight. I suppose I can get myself some clean clothes. These ones do look a little tatty.'

'And maybe we can leave Ruby with you, Bilfred? She can keep you company and you can tell her all about your story and the garden,' said Anna. 'I think she'll be safer here than anywhere else.'

'Of course. Would you like me to show you around, Ruby?' said Bilfred. 'You might be able to teach me a thing or two.'

'I'd love to,' Ruby said, clapping her hands with joy.

'Ruby, Bilfred can *speak* to the animals and plants,' said Jimmy.

'Oh, I know,' said Ruby. 'I've already heard him.'

'What do you mean?' asked Billy.

'Over there, he was talking to the sunflowers, which were telling him about the bees. They're thinking of swarming; there's a new queen on the horizon,' said Ruby.

Bilfred nodded, smiling. 'She's right, you know.'

'Then, over there, the lizards were saying that the compost heap needs turning,' Ruby continued.

'Right again,' said Bilfred, chuckling. 'You understand the garden almost as well as me, Ruby.'

Just as Billy was trying to blow away a bug, Ruby said, 'And Billy, bugs and animals are always drawn to you because they can feel your kindness, your loving heart – they love your vibration.'

'Oh! I just always find it really annoying!' Billy replied.

'Don't be annoyed, it's a compliment!' said Bilfred. 'I always told you you were special and that's why.'

'Ever since I was a little girl, I was always able to feel what people were thinking,' explained Ruby. 'And I can feel it even more with plants and animals. My

mum always told me that's the indigenous way –
our ancestors used lots of different methods of
communicating to survive in the Outback.'

'What's on the menu then, Bilfred?' Billy asked. He
could always sniff out something delicious.

'Wilfred and I are having some bies. I like bread,
and he likes pies . . .' Bilfred said, gesturing to his
brother.

'Put 'em together and we've made bies: a bread
pie!' Wilfred finished. 'Want some?'

'Sounds delicious, but we've just had some fish
and chips, so I'm pretty stuffed, but thank you,' said
Billy. Anna, Jimmy and Andy also shook their heads,
full up from their chippy feast.

When Bilfred and Wilfred had enjoyed their meal
together, the kids and Wilfred got themselves ready.
After cuddles, byes and cries – with many a sob from
Bo at the thought of Wilfred leaving for longer than
an hour – Anna opened up a tear to where they'd left
their bikes on the edge of the woods and they all
stepped through.

Chapter 14
Red's Reality

It was very hot in Alice Springs. And the heat wasn't helping Scary Red's furious temper. She couldn't believe she had been tricked by those pesky children, and now she was stuck here.

She had managed to give that silly little girl's family and the police the slip, her anthisalite-powered shoes giving her the edge. But they were still after her, relentless in their search, and she could always hear them in the distance as the group got bigger and bigger.

But, worse still, every hour that she went without her Nutrition Perfection and Youth-In-A-Bottle, Red could feel herself getting older, more tired, and as she

touched her skin it felt wrinkly, saggier, thinner . . .
she was disgusted! She *had* to find her way back to
her house before it was too late.

Scary Red had spent the night camped out by
the Todd River, keeping out of sight of the search
parties. But her old instincts of needing food and
drink were kicking in now she wasn't getting her
daily dose, and as things seemed to have quietened
this morning, she took a risk and broke cover to
take a drink by the river and cool herself from the
awful heat.

She bent over to scoop up the water in her hands,
but as she did so she caught a reflection of herself.
She screamed, a high-pitched blood-curdling sound
that echoed around the valley, and all of nature
seemed to flinch. She touched her face, unable to
believe that the wrinkled old lady reflected back could
really be her. She had held off the march of time for
well over a hundred years, and now . . .

A single teardrop hit the water. She hadn't cried in
a long, long time. The woman of steel had been
broken by a wrinkle.

'I look like . . . my mother,' she whispered, horror-struck.

In that moment, her mind took her back to being fifteen, sitting at the kitchen table with her mother and grandmother in their house in Poplar, London.

'How you present yourself, Betsy, how you look,' her grandmother was telling her, 'that's all that matters in this world. That's how you'll make something of yourself. Your beauty is your gift, it's what you can offer the world.'

'But I've got big ideas,' young Red replied. 'And I want people to listen to them, not just think about what I look like.'

Her mother laughed. 'Look pretty and find yourself a husband,' she told her daughter. 'And make sure he's got money if you want a happy marriage. No man wants a know-it-all; keep those big ideas to yourself.'

'And you need to get married while you're young, before you turn from a peach into a prune,' her grandmother said.

'What about love?' she asked innocently.

Both grandmother and mother squealed with laughter.

'Marriage isn't about love, that's a fairy tale. It's enough to have a roof over your head and food in your mouth,' her grandmother said.

'Anyway, you can't trust men – one minute you're married, the next minute they're gone,' said her mother.

'Yes, the only person in your life who you can trust is yourself – and me and your mother, of course,' her grandmother added.

'Which is why you need to look after us,' said her mother. 'Save us from the workhouse.'

'Well, I've got a job now, Mother,' said Betsy. 'In

that big building at Westminster, the Royal Institution. So I'll be bringing home money, I don't need to rely on a husband.'

'Pah! Money? What, ten shillings a week? What use is that? Don't waste your time and youth,' her mother scoffed.

Red blinked at her reflection in the river. It had been so long since she'd thought of her family. How foolish she had been to not listen to her grandmother and mother – youth and beauty were what mattered most.

Another memory came: she was older, twenty perhaps, and still at the Royal Institution. She remembered the feeling of being around people inventing medicines, making exciting discoveries, and changing the world. Men in white coats, using words she didn't understand, walking everywhere with purpose and excited about various strange and wonderful projects happening in different corners of the vast building.

She wasn't part of those exciting inventions, of course, but as a cleaner and someone who had to deal with the filth, she became very good at solving problems and making them disappear. And she loved it. The only thing she couldn't abide was the white uniform – instead she always wore her favourite colour, earning her the nickname 'Red'.

While most of what happened in that place she didn't understand, they paid just enough and on time, although even that was never enough for her mother and grandmother. They always wanted more. They told her over and over of their disappointment that she still hadn't found a husband yet, reminding her that her looks would fade. They filled her head with the idea that even her job at the Royal Institution had probably only been given to her because of how she looked, and surely once she had a wrinkle she'd be out of a job, with no money. But she wouldn't listen to them – not then.

Curse them, Red thought as she gazed at her reflection, *they were right*.

Her mind flitted to a few years later, twenty-four now and still at the bottom of the ladder even though she'd applied for job after job at the Institution. Her heart had become bitter and angry at the men in white coats who had once seemed so wonderful and clever, but now seemed petty and ridiculous. She had better ideas than lots of them, she knew she did, but they went unheard and ignored, just as her mother and grandmother had told her they would.

But then . . . one day she heard whispers in the building. An area of study that had made the discovery of the century: a perfectly formed pyramid-shaped blue stone that glinted whichever way you turned it. A scientist named Mr Tray had returned from Egypt with the crystal and was talking of using it to rip through the air and travel to different places, different times, even. It sounded like impossible magic to Red – but she was intrigued by the scientists' buzzing excitement. They were working day and night to unleash its power. Eventually they succeeded. And that's when Red's life changed.

'We're looking for a volunteer to help with an experiment,' her boss had called out to all the cleaners one morning. 'Whoever steps forward will be rewarded well.'

Without hesitation Red took a step. The chance to be part of science rather than just cleaning was too great to miss, and 'rewarded well' must have meant extra money, so perhaps that would get her mother and grandmother to leave her alone for a while.

The very next morning, she walked into a plain, white laboratory.

'We just need you to stand here,' a scientist explained to her, pointing at a cross marked on the centre of the floor in black. 'Then, when we tell you, walk forward. Give it one minute then come back.'

'What do you mean, "come back"?' Red asked in confusion.

'You'll understand when the time comes,' he replied dismissively. 'Ready?'

Red didn't know then that the scientists were worried that stepping through the rip into another world could alter your body forever, or even kill you! They just needed someone to test it on.

Red nodded and stepped on to the cross. She watched, curious, as one scientist held a staff with a crystal mounted on it. The man became calm, still

and focused, whispering to himself with his eyes
shut. Then the crystal began to spin, faster and faster
until it created a mirror image of itself, then he
pulled apart the two pyramids to reveal a tear in the
air – inside the tear seemed to be another place.
As she looked closer, Red gasped as she realized
it was an incredible forest. The rumours were true –
here was the rip in the air that led to a whole other

place, and Red was going to be the first to experience it!

Remembering her instructions, she cautiously stepped through the window. She found herself in the most beautiful woodland, full of exotic trees and plants – a far cry from the dirty streets of London she'd left behind. She picked juicy, rainbow-coloured ripe fruit from a tree, smelt multicoloured flowers the size of a bus and breathed in fresh, clean air, probably for the first time in her life. When she counted that a minute had passed, she walked back through the tear to the laboratory to an incredible round of applause from the excited scientists.

They gathered around Red, poking and prodding her, checking her heart rate and prising open her eyelids to make sure she was still in one piece. Then they took the rainbow-coloured fruit out of her hands to examine it, and whisked off, leaving her on her own in the middle of the room. Red smiled proudly.

In the following weeks, the experiments became bigger and more regular. At first she returned to the same forest, bringing back more samples of the plant

life and nature with her, but then Red was sent to different places, instructed to bring more and more back, to spend more time in the worlds she stepped into. She started to feel different . . . important, needed, powerful.

Then, on the day Red turned twenty-five, she was asked a question that no one had ever asked her before, a question that would change her whole life. Mr Tray, the scientist who had found the tetrahedron, asked, 'What do you want more than anything else in the world, Red?'

'I want to stay young forever,' she replied without hesitation.

He laughed and nodded. 'I can make that wish come true,' he said. 'But if I do, then I need something from you. Red, the Institution wants to shut down my studies. They say it's too dangerous. Too reckless.'

Red gasped. The world had been opened up to her and now it was being taken away?

'My dream is to create the perfect world, but to do that we need science, no matter what, to always win. Mother Nature, which is brutal and aggressive, often complicates things, making situations more difficult than they need to be,' Mr Tray said. 'So we need to take control. But many people would not agree, so I'm going to lead a group of scientists somewhere else – a place I'm going to call Terra Nova - where interfering people will no longer hold us back.'

'So what do you need from me?' Red asked. 'I'm not a scientist, where do I fit in?'

'We will need someone to take care of certain, er, problems, and that, young lady, is where you come in. I've seen how you operate here. Come with me, fix my problems, and in return I'll give you everlasting youth. So, what do you say? New life in a new world? Be young forever? And help humanity thrive like it never has before? I promise we'll look after your family . . . What have you got to lose?' he said.

Nothing, she thought to herself.

'I've already found the perfect location for Terra Nova,' he told her. 'The forest you visited on that very first experiment. It's remote and, from the samples you've brought back with you, it has an unusually rich and unique soil.'

'Why does the soil matter?' Red asked.

'Perfect nutrition,' he replied. 'I need the best soil to create plants that will feed people who live in Terra Nova with exactly the right nutrition for logical thinking. Which is why I need you. I want to put you in charge of producing the food needed by my city.

'You need to fulfil this duty for Terra Nova with no questions asked. Whatever it takes to provide the city with the very best. Nothing must get in the way of progress; nothing must spoil the dream.'

'And you can make me young forever?' Red asked. 'If I just help grow some vegetables?'

Mr Tray then held up a vial of liquid. 'Youth-In-A-Bottle. Maybe the most valuable thing on earth, but only for a chosen few.'

Red gazed at the glistening liquid. 'Does it really work?'

'How old do you think I am?' Mr Tray asked.

'Thirty-six, thirty-seven?'

He laughed. 'I'm seventy-two! And I've never felt better,' he said proudly. 'You wouldn't believe how many laws I have to break to make this. But laws are for the weak and stupid. My cause is more important.'

Red reached for the vial, but Mr Tray pulled his hand away.

'You'll receive one a week as payment, as long as you fulfil your role. If you fail, then the payment will stop.'

'And what happens if I don't take the vial?'

He looked at her firmly. 'It's better not to ask. The vial IS your payment, and you'll get it every week and you'll stay young every week. As long as you keep working, and look after Terra Nova and me, I will give you a life you've only dreamt of, and you'll stay just as you are. Forever!'

Red paused. Eternal youth. Being part of something bigger, something important. She reached for the vial again and took it from Mr Tray's hand. This was her chance to escape. To have everything she could ever want . . .

Another teardrop fell into the river, bringing Red back to the present.

Behind her she heard the noise of people making their way through the undergrowth. Quickly, she stood up from the river's edge and returned to her hiding place. As she crouched down low, Red noticed the ache in her joints. Her limbs felt heavy and old. Her rage grew again, and the fire in her belly – fuelling her need to return to her true self, her younger, beautiful self – was greater than ever. She had never been more determined; how *dare* they do this to her?

She knew the girl would want to bring back the child she had stolen, and it might not be long before they mastered the tetrahedron to open a tear to do just that.

So, perhaps now all she needed to do was to keep alert and wait. Then she would have her revenge.

Chapter 15

Wilfred's Return

As the kids and Wilfred headed through the village and towards the Green Giant pub, they heaved a sigh of relief that it wasn't absolutely crawling with police. There were still a few, but not enough to notice the kids coming back.

'Blimey, it's a bit quieter than when we left, isn't it? I can only see a couple of police officers now,' Andy said, pointing to people in uniform under a tree, 'and they're asleep!'

'Yeah, it would've been tricky otherwise,' Billy admitted.

'Are you ready, Mr Revel?' Jimmy asked.

'I don't know. I'm a bit nervous to be honest. You

know, I'm not the same person I was just a few weeks
ago,' the old man said. 'I've found my brother now –
but how can I tell anyone when I know Bilfred can
never come back? And I don't know quite what to
say about the fact I'm going to be leaving for
good again.'

Andy then started saying quietly:

If you can keep your head when all about you
    Are losing theirs and blaming it on you,
If you can trust yourself when all men doubt you,
    But make allowance for their doubting too;
If you can wait and not be tired by waiting,
    Or being lied about, don't deal in lies,
Yours is the Earth and everything that's in it,
    And – which is more – you'll be a Man, my son!

Everyone stood in stunned silence. 'Where did that
come from?' Billy asked.

'My mum likes a bit of poetry – must've sunk in,'
he replied.

'Well, I love it,' said Wilfred.

'We'll say we found you at the bus stop, like you'd just got back from being away or something. Then you can make up a story, anything you like,' said Anna.

'Make up a story?' said Wilfred, bewildered. 'I haven't done that for, well, ever.'

'News spreads fast once it hits the pub,' Billy said. 'So at least you'll only have to tell people once and the village gossip will do the rest!'

They walked up to the pub and all the kids looked expectantly at the old man. Wilfred took a deep breath and nodded. 'OK,' he said. 'I'll wait here until you give me the signal.'

Billy's mum and dad were behind the bar as usual, but the kids were surprised to see Anna's, Jimmy's and Andy's parents as well.

'Billy! Where have you been, and what have you been up to?' Billy's mum said, spotting them in the doorway. 'We've been worried sick!'

'We thought you were all going to holiday club, then spending the night at each other's houses,' Anna's dad said, sounding just as cross. 'But you weren't, were you? Jimmy's parents got a weird phone

message supposedly from Andy, but for some reason talking to them as if they were his mum.'

The friends looked at each other. They'd been rumbled! Clearly, relying on Johnny Perks hadn't been the best plan . . .

'Where were you all last night?' Andy's mum said. 'The truth!'

'Well, it's kind of complicated . . .' Billy started.

'We're all listening,' said Billy's dad. 'And I don't

266

want any lies. No mucking about, no exaggerating!'

'Look, we need to know you're safe, Billy,' his mum said, more gently now. 'When you say you're staying somewhere, we believe you. But now we've found out you've been lying to us it makes things difficult. Do you understand?'

'I know, and I didn't want to lie to you,' Billy began. 'But . . . sometimes you have to avoid telling the whole truth, because the thing you're trying to protect is bigger than you.'

The parents looked confused.

All the kids looked at Billy. Was it time to come clean? He took a deep breath. 'Earlier this year, me, Jimmy, Anna and Andy, we found a –'

At that moment a familiar voice piped up, 'An unhappy grandad, that's what they found!' Billy's grandad said, appearing from nowhere. 'I was feeling a little bit sad, a bit lonely without Betty.' His voice began to wobble, and he looked up at the sky.

'I know, Dad, I miss Mum, too,' said Billy's mum, walking over to give her dad a hug.

'Billy and his friends have been ever so kind, doing

everything they can to look after me. Cleaning, baking, keeping me company,' he continued. 'So I let them practise camping in my back garden. You shouldn't be telling them off. You've all done an amazing job raising these kids; they're kind, hard-working and conscientious.'

'Oh, stop it, Ted, that's so kind of you to say,' said Anna's mum, glowing red with pride – a second mum had now been won over by Grandad. 'We shouldn't have doubted you, Anna; now I feel bad. It's not OK to lie about where you are, but I suppose I can let it go this time because it sounds like you were just being kind.'

'But what I don't understand, Billy, is why you didn't tell us you were looking after Grandad? We wouldn't have been cross,' his mum said.

'Again, my fault,' Grandad jumped to Billy's defence. 'I didn't want them telling you or you'd only worry about me.'

'And, well, that's not the only secret we've been keeping,' Billy said sheepishly, and the parents groaned. 'We've also found a certain missing person at the bus stop.' Anna gave Wilfred the signal to walk into the pub.

'Hello, everyone,' Wilfred said. The pub fell silent. 'Ummm, it seems that I might have caused a bit of trouble for everyone without realizing? I'm ever so sorry. I never meant to cause alarm.'

After a second, the pub erupted in cheers and applause and people shouting 'WHERE HAVE YOU BEEN?', 'WHAT HAPPENED?', 'WE THOUGHT YOU'D BEEN BURGLED?', 'WE THOUGHT YOU'D VANISHED!', 'I THOUGHT YOU WERE DEAD.'

Then Billy's mum rang the bell behind the bar. 'Everyone, quiet in my pub! Let the man speak!' she shouted.

The bar fell silent.

'Now, Wilfred!' Billy's mum said. 'We've been really worried. Where on earth have you been?'

'I decided to go on a little holiday,' he said. 'I . . . Ummm . . . Well, on my big birthday I got a free bus pass, didn't I? And I wanted to celebrate and get out of the village.'

'You went on holiday? But you've been gone for

weeks?!' Billy's dad said. 'And you left the back door open, someone's been in and there was cash all over the floor . . .'

'I was in a hurry. I knocked over my piggy bank,' Wilfred explained. 'I took the bigger coins, but I was in such a rush to get the 11:30 a.m. from Little Alverton to Lavenham, I had to leave the rest.'

'Then where did you go, darlin'?' Billy's mum asked, coaxing him to tell them more.

'Well, from Lavenham I got the 12:45 p.m. to Leigh-on-Sea, then I took a long stroll to Southend. I had a lovely time,' Wilfred continued, getting into his stride. 'I got myself some fish and chips –'

'I hope you got some gravy with that,' someone interrupted.

'No, I'm strictly a ketchup and tartar sauce man – none of that funny business! Then I had to fight off some seagulls who tried to steal me chips.' Everyone in the pub chuckled knowingly. 'I watched the ships go up the estuary, chatted to some fishermen and . . . well . . . I met someone,' Wilfred said, looking all bashful. There was a pause, then everyone erupted again in whoops and cheers.

'I knew it!' said one of the regulars in the pub. 'I said he'd either fallen off a cliff, got kidnapped or found love. Well, if anyone needs it, it's you, you grumpy old man,' he said, laughing.

'Yeah, let's just say I'm not grumpy any more. That sneaky peck on the cheek has put a big smile on my face,' Wilfred said to more cheers. 'The only thing is she does live a distance away, so you might not see that much of me from now on,' Wilfred said, pleased that he'd given himself a brilliant excuse for spending lots of time with Bilfred.

'Rein it in a bit, Wilfred,' Anna whispered, echoing what the rest of the children were thinking.

'You kinda put me on the spot,' Wilfred whispered back, out of the corner of his mouth. 'Love is the only thing that will shut them up. And anyway, I did find my long-lost love – my brother.'

'Come on, Mr Revel, why don't I get you a drink?' said Billy's dad. 'You can fill us in on your adventure.'

'Good idea!' said Billy, seeing their chance to escape the grown-ups and their interrogation – it seemed Wilfred's arrival had made them forget the kids were in trouble – and start the next part of their plan. 'Sounds like BORING adult talk, so we'll leave you to it!'

Mr Revel looked helplessly at Billy, who shrugged. 'Maybe I should be getting home . . .'

'Nonsense!' Billy's mum said. 'Come on, have a drink on the house so you can tell us all about this mystery lady of yours.'

Billy nudged his friends. 'We're going to the treehouse, Mum!' They didn't wait for an answer and ran outside.

Chapter 16

The Big Idea

Once they'd clambered up into the treehouse, the kids flopped down.

'What on earth just happened?' Billy asked the others. 'My grandad just completely saved us.'

'Yeah, I wonder why he did that?' Anna agreed. 'Do you think he knows something?'

'But what?' Andy said.

'Well, he's in the pub now and will be stuck there for some time if the chaos we left is anything to go by,' Billy said. 'So I suppose we'll have to wait to ask him.'

'In the meantime, let's get on with our other mission – getting our plan together to solve the mystery of the stolen children,' said Jimmy. 'Now we know what's been going on, we've got to do something.'

'Jimmy's right,' said Billy. 'We should pull together all the information we need to give to Jerry Draper, so he can crack on with finding the families of these Giants and break the story about Scary Red, so she can be stopped.'

'Guys, I've been thinking – we need to be really careful,' said Anna. 'This will almost certainly be the biggest child-kidnapping story in history. The whole world is going to want to know about this – and that's attention we don't need around the woods.'

'Anna's right,' Billy agreed. 'The Myas wouldn't be happy if we did anything to expose the magic in Waterfall Woods. And we already decided that if anyone else from our world found out about the power of anthisalite it would be a disaster.'

'So, what do we do?' Jimmy said.

'What if we only give Jerry Draper the details of the Giants who would still have living family? We owe that to them,' said Anna. 'Billy, do you think you could find that out from the cube?'

'I can try . . .' He took out the white cube from his

backpack and pulled up various graphs and lists, until he found one that showed the Top Trumps-style information about the Giants that they'd seen Scary Red look at in her house. 'Look, here are the ages of the Giants. It looks like most were stolen around 150 years ago, then it slows down a lot. I'd guess there are probably only ten to fifteen Giants that would still have living families in our world?'

'So, we get all the info together on those Giants,' said Anna. 'Where they came from, how old they were when they were stolen. Then if we share this with Jerry, hopefully he can help piece their stories together.'

'Right, sounds like a plan!' Andy said.

The kids got to work, collating everything into a collage of information for each Giant. Billy left the writing to the others, while he used his best skill – thinking of things in a different way – and found his *Encyclopedia Britannica* so he could cut out maps and pictures to build up mini files to help bring their stories to life. Then he took Polaroid pictures of the projection of the Giants' faces and stuck them to the maps.

They raided Billy's mum's office for a large manila envelope and put everything inside. Just like the first time they'd given Jerry a scoop, they sealed it with some wax from a candle and stamped it with the Queen's head from a penny.

'Now that looks official!' said Billy.

'Which reminds me, do I need to be Ron Bond again?' asked Jimmy. 'I did like it before, even though it's quite nerve-wracking.'

'Yes!' Anna said. 'Jerry will trust you because the last story about the evil farmer and his polluting factory became a big scoop. Don't worry – you'll be brilliant.'

'OK, you all go to a payphone to make the call,' said Andy. 'I'll hang back here at the pub and hand the envelope to Jerry when you're done.'

'We'll give you a signal on the walkie-talkie from the phone box,' said Billy.

'And I'll just say a man in an Aston Martin gave this to me, same as last time,' replied Andy.

Billy, Anna, Andy and Jimmy all snuck down the stairs and back through the pub. Things had calmed down considerably since they left, although Wilfred was only just making his excuses to leave.

'OK, well, thank you all so much, but I think I'll be off home now,' said Wilfred.

'Can I come back with you, Wilfred?' Grandad asked. 'I think we have a lot to catch up on.'

'That would be lovely, Ted,' Wilfred agreed.

'Before you go, could I just have one picture of you, Mr Revel?' Jerry Draper asked the old man. 'So I can celebrate your brilliant story in the local paper.'

'Of course,' said Wilfred, who was starting to enjoy

a little bit of attention, then he headed home with Grandad.

Billy, Anna and Jimmy went outside to the phone box opposite, while Andy hung back in the bar.

In the phone box, Jimmy closed his eyes and started breathing deeply.

'What are you doing, Jimmy?' Billy asked. 'Do you feel ill?'

'I'm channelling Ron, aren't I? I need to get into character,' Jimmy replied.

Billy and Anna looked at each other and raised their eyebrows.

'Whatever makes you happy,' Anna said, hiding a smile.

After a couple of minutes, Jimmy announced, 'Right, I'm ready.' They dialled the number.

'Hello, the Green Giant pub, how can I help you?' Billy's mum's sing-song voice came through the receiver.

'I need to speak to Jerry Draper,' Jimmy said in a low, posh voice. 'I have a very important message for him.'

'Wait, I recognize your voice. Is this Ron Bond again?' Billy's mum said. 'Do you have another special job for our Jerry?'

Jimmy looked panicked. 'Don't let her put you off!' Billy muttered.

'Er, sorry. I can neither confirm nor deny. I'll only speak to Jerry,' Jimmy said.

'Oh, I love the drama. Let me get him for you darlin',' she said, turning to Jerry. 'Jerry, put that Scotch egg down and pick up this call.'

'Hello? Jerry Draper speaking,' he said, his mouth still half full of his favourite bar snack.

'This is your informant, Ron Bond. I have another story for you,' Jimmy/Ron said.

'Really?' said Jerry. 'Things have turned a corner for me since our last scoop – people actually take me seriously as a journalist!'

'This is even bigger than before,' said Jimmy/Ron.

'Bigger? Gordon Bennett! What is it now? Another rogue farmer? A serial thief?' Jerry asked, intrigued.

'Jerry, in life it's important to know when to talk and when to listen, and now is a time to listen.' Jimmy put his hand over the receiver and mouthed to Billy and Anna: 'That's what my teacher always used to say!'

'Yes! I'm all ears,' said Jerry excitedly.

'You proved yourself to be a great . . . um . . . asset last time. And now I've got quite the story. It's a global child-snatching ring.'

'Child-snatching? Global?' replied Jerry. 'What do you mean? How many kids are we talking – four, five?'

'Hundreds – going back many years,' Jimmy/Ron replied.

'Are you having me on? A child-snatching

conspiracy? Without anyone doing anything? Impossible,' Jerry said.

'It's not a conspiracy. We know who has been snatching these children and why – what we need you to do is get more information on the most recently snatched children. This person has never been caught before because no one could join the dots, but I believe you could be the man to do it, Jerry Draper.'

'Well, I am a pretty good journalist,' said Jerry, sounding very pleased with himself. 'OK, what evidence do you have?'

'The agency has a pack of information for you, which should be more than enough to get you on the right track, then you need to do your job! A boy from the village is going to give it to you now. You are to speak to no one about this – including the landlady of the pub!'

'Yes, I-I understand,' Jerry replied seriously.

When Jimmy put the phone down, Billy announced on his walkie-talkie, **'Deliver the package, Pie. Over!'**

'It's on!' replied Andy, and he belted over to Jerry and shoved the envelope into his hands. 'I've been told to give this to you by a tall, muscly man called Ron in a very posh car. He said you'd know what it was for. He also said to pull yourself together and stop percrustinating.'

'It's PROcrastinate – and OK, thank you,' Jerry replied.

Before he could be asked any more questions, Andy rushed off to join the others, but Billy's mum had other ideas.

'Andy,' she shouted after him, 'do you want some sarnies, love? Or there are some Cornish pasties fresh from the oven?'

Andy couldn't resist a fresh pasty. 'Yes, please, Mrs Palmer,' he quickly replied.

'Well, go and get the rest of the gang then, Andy – I want you to sit down over there and have some tea, so you've got some food inside you.'

'Yes, Mrs Palmer,' he said, and dashed out to get the others. As soon as they came back in, they were presented with a tray of four Cornish pasties, each with a little green salad on the side.

'Wow! Dad's Cornish pasties – my favourite,' said

Billy, who couldn't resist the crumbly, buttery pastry, filled with perfectly seasoned slices of beef, turnip, onion and potato.

'Right, kids, be careful, they're hot inside,' said Billy's mum. 'Want any sauces with that? I've got brown sauce, Gentleman's Relish, English mustard, French mustard, wholegrain mustard, but NO ketchup, not with Cornish pasties – that's for heathens.'

All the kids shouted, 'ENGLISH MUSTARD, PLEASE!'

As she came back with the yellow condiment, Billy said 'Wait!', and rummaged around in his backpack, before pulling out a large plastic syringe from his Meccano set.

'What are you going to do with that?' Anna asked, utterly bemused.

'You just wait – this is genius,' he replied. He stuck the syringe in the mustard, sucked up some sauce, then pushed it into the Cornish pasty, squeezing in some of the golden goodness. 'Why dip in the mustard when you can stuff it?' he said with a grin.

'Fair point, Billy!' Jimmy replied, before they all took it in turns to load their Cornish pasties – apart from Andy, who said English mustard goes up his nose and makes him cry.

They all devoured the hand-held deliciousness.

'Right, we'd better get going, guys,' Billy said, wiping his mouth. 'Mum! You OK if we go to see Grandad?'

'Course you can, my loves,' she replied, 'as long as that *is* where you're going?'

'Yes, it is, Mrs Palmer,' replied Andy, with the most angelic face.

And, with that, they jumped on their bikes and whizzed off to Wilfred Revel's house.

Chapter 17
The Wise Man

When they arrived at Wilfred's cottage, they found Grandad and Wilfred sitting at the kitchen table, having an intense conversation.

'Grandad, what's going on?' Billy said breathlessly. 'How come you saved our bacon? We were about to get in so much trouble!'

The old man looked at each of the kids, stopping at Billy, and said, 'I *KNOW.*'

'What do you mean, you know?' Billy replied, confused.

'Come on, kids, don't be silly. *I know,*' he said again. 'I know what you've discovered in those woods. I've known since you asked me about the Rhythm,

285

Billy. I told you the woods had dark secrets, but it seems you ignored me and have been going in there anyway. Wilfred has filled me in on everything.'

'Grandad, I had no idea you were on to us,' said Billy. 'But if you're so cross, why did you cover for us?'

'I covered up for you because I believe you were doing what you thought was best. And now, from what Wilfred tells me, things have gone too far. Whatever is happening in that other world needs to stop. Finish whatever it is you need to do and put an end to it, once and for all.'

'How do you know about the woods?' Anna asked.

'I've always known the woods aren't quite what they seem. Ever since Bilfred went missing all those years ago. Back then, Wilfred and I were best mates,' said Grandad. He turned to Wilfred. 'You don't know this, but I followed you and your brother that fateful night.'

'You did?' Wilfred said, clearly surprised.

'No way!' Andy said. 'You saw it all? The eye sucking and everything?'

'Well, I tried to follow, but you and Bilfred vanished into thin air,' Grandad said. 'So, I waited and then watched as you came running out of the woods with one eye missing. You collapsed and I was so frightened. I dragged you to the road where my parents could help you. I've been very wary of the woods ever since.'

'I never knew that,' Wilfred said, a tear forming in his eye at the thought of that day.

'Nothing was ever the same,' Grandad said, shaking his head. 'At first it was my mum who told me to stay away from you, then, by the time things blew over, you didn't want to talk to me – every time I tried, you ignored me.'

'I only ignored you because you ignored me,' Wilfred said. 'I was cross with you.'

'Do you remember when we used to rearrange all the farmer's hay bales from the haystack, making a labyrinth of tunnels all the way through them?' Grandad reminisced, chuckling. 'Well, until that time you got chased out by a massive rat!'

'I do remember!' Wilfred said, laughing too. 'And going scrumping for those really ugly, wonky apples from Mrs O'Reilly's orchard that were the most delicious things in the world. We ate so many one time that we both ended up with terrible stomach ache.'

'Oh! What about that time we thought we'd seen a ghost in her barn, but then realized it was a big old owl!' Grandad grinned. 'We were so scared!'

'And do you remember that time I drew a frog on your face? It wouldn't come off, no matter how much we scrubbed, and then you had to go to your brother's christening! Your parents were so cross!' Wilfred said, and they both laughed their heads off.

Grandad wiped a tear from his cheek. 'Nostalgia is painful sometimes, isn't it, Wilf?' he said, looking at his old friend. 'Makes you realize how good it was back then and how much we lost by not being friends. It's silly, really, that these arguments travel into adulthood. All because people are too proud and scared to say sorry – but I *am* sorry, old friend. I really am.'

'Me too,' Wilfred agreed. 'I've missed you.' He turned to the kids. 'This story was never finished, and it needed youngsters like you to sort it out. Thank you. It's good to reunite with my friend. It means I can go and live with my brother without any unfinished business.'

'What do you mean "with your brother"?' Grandad asked.

'It seems you don't quite know everything, Grandad,' said Billy. And, over the course of a pot of tea and packet of Rich Tea biscuits, the kids and Wilfred explained more.

'So, all this time, Bilfred has been stuck in those woods?' said Grandad. 'That's awful.'

'It's a relief just to tell someone else the truth,' said Andy.

'Well, if we're talking about the truth, then perhaps I should tell you that I *have* visited those magical woods. Just once,' Grandad said.

'When?' Billy asked. 'Tell us exactly what happened.'

Grandad explained. 'A couple of days ago, when all those police were here looking for Wilfred, I saw you kids all run into the woods. First Billy, Jimmy and Anna and then, later, Andy, who was being followed by that Bruno boy. Now, I know you boys don't get on, so I wanted to check that everything was OK. By the time I'd got to the edge of the woods, I saw Bruno, just as he walked through a shimmering haze, and I couldn't help myself: I went through it, too. That's when I realized I wasn't in the normal woods any more – it felt extraordinary, magical! I tried to catch up with Bruno, and that's when I then saw him getting snatched by . . .'

'A flying robot?' Jimmy asked.

'Yes!' said Grandad.

'That was a Ranger,' Jimmy explained. 'A robot soldier that does exactly what Scary Red says.'

'Well, it scared the life out of me. I knew I was out of my depth, too old to be of use. Besides, I had no idea where any of you were, so I just hoped that you knew what you were doing, and I made my way home as quickly as I could. I've been worried sick about you all ever since.

'I decided to give you twenty-four hours to come back yourselves, and then I would tell your parents. I just had a feeling that you wouldn't want me to break the secret of those woods. Anyway, I still remember what the newspapers were like all those years ago – no one believed Wilfred then because he was just a boy, so why would they believe me? They'd just think I was a foolish old man. So I just had to wait it out. Then you came back, thank goodness.'

'Grandad, you've been to Waterfall Woods!' Billy said in wonder. 'If you thought everything was incredible in that little bit, you ain't seen nothing yet! It's HUGE! Luckily we discovered these amazing flying buzzpacks so we can zip about easily. Oh, I can't wait to show you!'

'That place is something else,' Wilfred said. 'And I'll be going back there soon to live with Bilfred.'

'But we've only just reconnected,' said Grandad sadly. 'It's a shame for me, but I understand.'

'We'll take you into the woods to see Wilfred and Bilfred whenever you want, Grandad,' said Billy.

'So, how exactly do you get from here to the magical world?' Grandad asked.

'When you say the "shimmering haze", did you notice that big gnarly tree?' said Jimmy. Grandad nodded. 'Well, all you have to do is give it a great BIG hug and it opens and closes the gate,' Jimmy told him.

'You never would've guessed it, would you?' Grandad said in awe. 'Hugging a tree?'

'It's getting late, kids,' Mr Revel announced. 'And I think you should all go home and see your parents before it's dark. A good night of sleep and I can get back to my brother and you can take young Ruby home.'

'You're right,' said Billy. 'Mum and Dad will be watching me like a hawk now!'

'We'll meet at your grandad's tomorrow morning, bright and early, and I can use my new skills with Scary Red's tetrahedron to get us to Bilfred's garden in no time,' Anna suggested.

'Can I stay here for a bit, Wilfred?' Grandad asked. 'If you're about to vanish off into those woods for who knows how long, maybe forever, it might be nice to chat for a bit longer.'

'I'd love that,' Wilfred said. 'Seems like these kids have brought me back my brother and my best friend.' He smiled. After all these years, Wilfred Revel no longer felt alone.

Chapter 18

Ruby's Return

They all met at Grandad's house first thing the
following morning.

Anna had something special to show them. 'Guys,
look at this,' she said, bursting with pride. She pulled
the crystal out of her pocket and started to perform
the now familiar ritual in the palm of her hand, without
the need for the staff. The crystal spun and reflected
on itself right above her fingers.

'You're so good at this, Anna!' Jimmy said. 'Who
needs a bulky old staff!'

'I was just playing with it at home last night, and I
realized I could do it myself. It will make carrying it
around so much easier,' said Anna. They all stepped

through the window she had created into Bilfred's garden. A very happy Bilfred, Ruby, Basil and Chief Mirren were all having a tasty breakfast together.

As soon as the brothers set eyes on each other, Wilfred ran over to Bilfred, who pulled him in for a big hug. They had barely been apart for a day, but after a lifetime of being separated even the shortest of times felt like forever.

Bo came pelting out of the middle of the compost heap, covered in bits of rotting veg and flowers. 'I like you! I like you! It's good to have you back!' she said, giving Wilfred the warmest Boona welcome, complete with slobbery licks. Wilfred laughed.

Anna went over to Ruby and gave the little girl a squeeze.

'Hello, Ruby,' she said. 'Have you had fun with Bilfred?'

'Yes. I'm so glad I stayed for a bit longer. And I've learnt so much from the big old Giant – he's just awesome!' Ruby said.

'You're ready to go home now, though?' Anna asked.

'I'm ready. My parents and family will be *really* worried by now,' Ruby replied. Then she looked sad.

'What's the matter?' Anna asked gently.

'I think I'll miss you all,' Ruby said. 'Do you think I'll ever be able to come back?'

'I don't know why, but I have a feeling this won't be the last time we see each other,' Anna said.

Chief Mirren flew over and whispered in Anna's ear. Anna nodded in agreement, with a smile on her face, then Chief Mirren went to a chest she had brought with her. She fluttered back with a flint necklace in her hand.

'Ruby, you are an unexpected treasure joining our family,' Chief Mirren said. 'I'm sure Anna is right that this shall not be the last time we all meet. And, to help with that promise, I have a gift for you. Open your hand.'

Ruby held out her hand. Chief Mirren placed a perfectly smooth piece of flint in her palm, complete with twine.

'For me?' Ruby asked. 'What is it?'

'It's a flint necklace, just like the one I have from the Sprites, Ruby,' Billy said. 'It means that if you ever need to contact us, you can.'

'Wow,' said Ruby, amazed, as she turned the flint round and round in her hands.

'Little Ruby, yous is one of us now!' Basil said. 'I've said it before, and I'll say it again: these stones keeps us all together. Yous is connected to us now, whether yous likes it or not, no matter where yous is,' he said, chuckling.

'In fact,' Chief Mirren announced, 'I think maybe the time has come for all of you to have your own necklaces. We only gift them to non-Sprites in very special circumstances. But I think this is one of those occasions.'

Anna returned the flint necklace that she had been wearing to Billy, as Basil tied her very own flint around her neck. He then flew over to Andy and Jimmy and did the same.

'I've always really wanted one of these,' Andy said.

'Remember, these are for times of emergency or real need,' warned Chief Mirren. 'Their magic is precious and shouldn't be overused.' Everyone looked at each other seriously and nodded.

'Ruby, before you go, I must remind you –' Chief Mirren started, but, before she could finish, Ruby interrupted her.

'Don't worry, I know – the secrets of these woods are safe with me.'

'Of course,' Chief Mirren said with a smile.

'You ready, Ruby?' Anna asked.

'Maybe I should come with you?' suggested Billy. 'So I can be useful and keep . . .'

'An eye on me?' Anna finished, giving him a look.

'Or I could wait here instead, because you'll do fine on your own,' said Billy shyly.

'Exactly,' said Anna.

'Just look out for Scary Red. She might be waiting for you,' Jimmy told her.

Anna screwed up her face in response. 'My guess is that she'll have run away by now,' she replied. 'And

even if she is there, what can she do without this?'
She pointed at the crystal. 'I'm not scared of her!'

Bilfred let out a sob and said to Ruby, 'Little one,
I know we've only had a short time together, but you
are truly marvellous. You've helped me fine-tune my
telepathy – trust your thoughts, eh? I'll send you
some feelings.'

'I'll dream you some songs,' Ruby replied.

Anna closed her eyes, took a deep breath and
started visualizing Alice Springs. The heat, the smells,
the homely street . . . The crystal began to spin and
split, then she pulled apart the two halves to create a
tear. The main road in Alice Springs came into view.

It was funny that, as the morning sun was rising in
Bilfred's garden, through the tear they could see the
most beautiful orange sunset, and the smell of the
land slowly cooling after a day of heat was
unmistakable. Ruby gasped as she realized home was
finally within reach. With one final wave goodbye, Ruby
took Anna's hand, and the two girls stepped through.
Whoosh! – the tear was closed, and
the girls were gone.

'I'm never going to want to travel any other way again,' Andy said, in wonder.

'I hope they'll be OK,' Billy muttered to himself, feeling uneasy.

'Come on, Billy. I thought you had decided to start trusting Anna to look after herself,' Jimmy said, an air of frustration in his voice.

'I know, I know,' said Billy. 'She's always OK.'

Ruby was beside herself with excitement as she skipped down her street with Anna. They stopped under a street lamp opposite Ruby's house, the sound of the evening chorus of bugs and crickets just getting into their noisy stride, echoing in the otherwise silent street.

'Are you going to be all right from here?' Anna asked Ruby gently.

'I'm gonna be fine,' said Ruby

confidently. 'You can't come with me anyway because people will only ask more questions, and that could get tricky. Besides, you need to get back to the boys – they need you.'

Anna nodded and said, 'Yes, that's true – we have a lot of mysteries still to solve about what's been going on. And we have to help the Rhythm.'

'Look after the Rhythm, and the Rhythm will look after you,' said Ruby.

'You really are the cleverest, wisest, cutest young lady I've ever met, Ruby,' Anna said, smiling.

'I know,' said Ruby.

'And humble,' continued Anna.

'I know,' repeated Ruby.

'And the smelliest,' Anna giggled.

'No, you are!' said Ruby, and they both laughed.

A light went on in a porch across the street, then a worried voice said: 'Ruby, is that you?'

Ruby smiled. 'Mum! It's me! I'm back!'

'Take care of yourself,' Anna whispered, as the two gave each other a big hug. 'Remember to use the flint if you need us.'

Ruby nodded and smiled at her friend before running across the street and into her elated mum's outstretched arms.

With a huge smile on her face, Anna walked back up the street that was just coming to life as porch light after porch light was turned on by locals wanting to find out what all the noise was about. The sound of 'She's back, Ruby's back!' was ringing in her ears as aunts, friends and neighbours ran to welcome Ruby home.

Anna headed to the spot where they had arrived and started to create the tear, calming her heart and focusing on visualizing Bilfred's garden in her mind. The crystal spun and split, and the window was created. With one final look back, Anna stepped confidently through.

With just milliseconds to go before the window closed, Scary Red came from out of nowhere and, powered by the stones in her shoes, whooshed through after Anna, falling into an exhausted

heap behind a tree.

'What was that?' Anna whipped her head round at the sound.

But, as she scanned the area, there was no sign of anyone. Anna shook her head. She was imagining things. She watched as the window closed, sighing with relief that the danger was over, then walked off in the direction of Bilfred's shed.

A smile crept across Scary Red's crepey, wrinkled face – she'd now missed her scheduled doses of Nutrition Perfection and Youth-In-A-Bottle, and it was starting to show.

Red was back in the world where she belonged, and now she would get her revenge. But first, she needed to reverse this 'horrifying' ageing process. She had vials at home, but didn't want to risk the children realizing she was back. Besides, missed vials meant faster ageing, and with each moment that passed she was getting older and older. She would need as much Youth-In-A-Bottle as she could get her hands on to put it right. So, instead of going home, she'd go to Terra Nova, speak to Mr Tray and beg for as much as she could get.

Making sure no one could spot her, she kicked off the ground and shot away to the big city.

On arriving at Terra Nova's entrance gate, Scary Red touched her watch to change back into her iconic flowing red dress, then positioned her face in front of the facial recognition device.

'Denied,' the machine said sternly.

She tried again.

'Denied,' the machine repeated.

It seemed her face had changed so much it was unrecognizable to the device.

'Select alternative identification method,' the machine said.

Scary Red chose Retinal Display from a list of options on the screen and held her face up to the device again.

A line scanned Red's eyes, then: 'Access granted,' the computer announced. On the screen, Scary Red's stats came up: Betsy Walker, GAMEKEEPER, age: 185.

'I do not need to be reminded,' she tutted, walking through the gate.

Scary Red rarely came to Terra Nova, preferring instead to remain in her own house in the woods. When she had first taken up her role, she had loved the bright, modern feel of the city that was so perfect it couldn't have been built by a human hand – it was a world apart from London's rowdy, noisy, smelly alleyways where she had grown up.

But she soon grew bored of the uniformity and missed the different types of people she would come across back home: artists, sailors, bakers, bankers, shopkeepers, actors, soldiers – life had felt more vibrant and exciting. The shine of Terra Nova faded as she realized how boring and predictable the place was; genius, yes, but dull nonetheless. It was too perfect, even for Scary Red.

Besides, Mr Tray and the other founders didn't want her there anyway. She knew too much, and would the people of Terra Nova really be willing to accept their utopia if they knew it came at the price of stolen children?

As she made her way through the streets, people openly stared at her in disgust; no one here looked over thirty, and her ageing face was out of place. Scary Red's anger rose again. It was because of her that Terra Nova even existed! It was *her* gardens that supported it all and created the Nutrition Perfection that everyone took to survive. Maybe it was time that she upped the price for her silence?

Soon enough she arrived at the founders' offices – a huge, towering, glass-fronted building. She went straight up to the front desk.

'I want to see Mr Tray,' she demanded.

The receptionist touched her ear, and listened for a second. 'Mr Tray will meet you in the Peace Room,' she said with a smile.

Scary Red glided down a tubular corridor that glistened like the inside of a shell, with whites, blues and silvers. On either side, she could see into other meeting rooms – they were occupied by men in important-looking white uniforms, who were pointing at projections that came from white cubes on the tables. It felt more like a hospital than an office. No smiles, no laughter, just focus and efficiency.

She arrived at the Peace Room – not that it felt that peaceful. It was slightly bigger than the other meeting rooms and had a long, intimidating table that dominated the space. She recognized the person standing at the other end and could feel his tension. Scary Red refused to sit; she was too angry.

After a moment's silence, Mr Tray screwed up his face and said, 'What on earth has happened to you? What have you done to yourself? You look hideous! You look . . . old.'

'There's been a breach,' Scary Red replied.

'What kind of breach? Is it containable?' he spat.

'It's five children, and yes, it's containable – I'll have it fixed.'

'Children? Well, Red, children are your speciality, so sort it. NOW. Whatever it takes.'

'These ones are particularly tricky. When I visited Australia to take a replacement grower, they tricked me and trapped me on the other side of a window without my staff and without Youth-In-A-Bottle. Luckily, I was able to get back here. Although they still have the tetrahedron.'

My Tray's face filled with fury, and for the first time Scary Red felt vulnerable and frightened. 'You've lost one of the most powerful, precious objects we own? There are only two stones in existence, you know that!' He took a breath. 'I cannot believe you've allowed this to happen,' he said coldly.

'Well, to make things right, I will need a few doses of Nutrition Perfection and Youth-In-A-Bottle. As soon as I'm refreshed, I'll have no problem overpowering these pathetic children and getting the tetrahedron back.'

'You've put everything at risk and now you ask me for help – perhaps I should just get rid of you.'

'You know exactly why you can't dispose of me,'

Scary Red snapped. 'Not only do I ensure the nutritional supply keeps coming – my gardens and growers feed you, feed everyone! – but I also keep your secret; no one knows it's stolen children that are powering your dream. So yes, I have made a mistake. Yes, I have underestimated these children. But I will fix it, like I've fixed every other mess. Write out a prescription for the vials I need and when I'm back to my usual, younger self I will put everything right.'

'I don't think you realize the effort it takes to make Youth-In-A-Bottle. It's the most valuable commodity we possess,' he said in a matter-of-fact tone. 'I can't give you more than your allowance. Your demise is your fault. I have always delivered on our original contract – your ageing is your problem.'

'You promised to keep me young forever,' Scary Red said. 'You're going back on that?'

Mr Tray was unfazed. '*You* promised you would run the gardens without any problems,' he told her. 'You also promised to keep your work secret. And yet here you are, causing a fuss about the fact that *you* have failed. You have just one job: to keep the wild out, so we can keep this dream alive. We have to be single-minded in our mission. You do not hold the power here; I do. I control the supply of Youth-In-A-Bottle, and therefore I control you.'

Red instantly deflated. She knew he was right: what little leverage she had was undermined by her need for Youth-In-A-Bottle.

He paused for a second, and his tone softened. 'I have always been very generous to you, Red, so I will grant you a new prescription for a double dose from our facility here, to help with your *current* situation.' He looked at her with disdain. 'But it won't be enough to reverse this process. You will never have the same youth you once did – it's too late.'

He pulled out a crisp, white prescription pad from a hidden drawer in the table and placed a jar of vivid blue ink next to it. He then took out the most incredibly colourful feather, with a nib cut into the quill, dipped it into the ink and wrote out the prescription.

For: Red
1 x box Nutrition Perfection;
2 x vials Youth-In-A-Bottle.
Signed: Mr Tray, The Founder

To the right of his signature, he left the nib on the paper so ink seeped out, then pressed his thumb into it, showing a fingerprint. 'There, done,' he said, putting the pen down next to the prescription and getting up. He waved his hand in front of the wall to reveal a beautiful round window that looked out over Terra Nova in all its beauty.

'This is why I need this problem fixed immediately, because the ultimate dream – this! – is much bigger than you, me or anyone else,' he said, staring at his creation. 'The technology that my scientists are working on will take us not only to a different place but a different time.'

While he was preoccupied with his 'dream', Scary Red took her chance, leant forward and silently grabbed the quill, putting an '0' next to the '2' for Youth-In-A-Bottle. Then she put the pen down exactly where she found it.

'So, fix it, now,' Mr Tray said, turning back to her. 'I
don't like things getting in the way of my plans
– that's why I created Terra Nova in the first place,
because I don't want rules governing me. I want to do
things how I want. Get rid of the children. Get back
the tetrahedron. Otherwise, there will be no more
Youth-In-A-Bottle for you at all.'

'I can fix it – although the Rhythm seems to be
bigger, stronger. I feel the woods are changing,' Scary
Red told him.

'We need the Rhythm to be strong, that's true, but
not too strong,' he said. 'Don't forget what happened
last time. We had to poison all those Giants and
eradicate the Sprites. It might not have been a
complete success, but at least it gave us more time,'
he said, through gritted teeth. 'Now, leave. You have a
job to do. Do not fail me again.'

Scary Red walked out, looking down at the
prescription in her hand and smiling smugly to herself.

She glided down the corridor, arrived at the
dispensary on the ground floor, and peered through
the window in the door; it was a small, sparse room

with a white counter topped with a small white cube, and a lone man stood behind it, wearing a very sharp white suit, not a hair out of place.

'Twenty?' the dispenser said with a shocked look on his face, as she handed over the prescription a moment later. 'This is most irregular. Why on earth would you need twenty Youth-In-A-Bottles? I've only ever given singles . . .'

'But you can see this has been signed by The Founder,' Red started, trying to contain her anger. 'Would you like me to bring him to you now? Tell him he's got it wrong?'

'No, that won't be necessary,' the dispenser replied, with fear on his face – Mr Tray's temper was legendary.

'So, do it, and quickly,' Red snapped.

'I can give you the Nutrition Perfection now – that is not a problem.' He opened a drawer in the wall and passed a box of orange vials across the counter.

Before he'd even blinked, Red had inserted one into her belly button. She closed her eyes and sighed as her aches and pains started to disappear, energy surged through her body and the hunger pangs subsided. She touched the white cube with her finger, projecting her stats. The numbers that started off flashing red changed to amber, then green; her blood pressure and heart rate returned to normal levels. Without hesitation she inserted the second.

'I only have six Youth-In-A-Bottle available,' he said, and swiped on the projection to pop open a drawer on the wall behind him. 'The rest are in the deep freeze and are reserved for The Founder. And we're not due a new delivery for several days.'

'Can't you get more?' Red demanded.

'No, I can't. We only have one supplier: this extraordinary woman of very few words, who is even scarier than you, but, my, is she enchanting . . .'

'Give me the six you have ready,' Red said, snapping him back to reality.

The dispenser reluctantly passed her the vials. Scary Red grabbed them greedily, immediately inserting one vial into her belly button and quickly changing it for a second as soon as it was drained, slipping the final four into her pocket. She had never taken more than one vial before and as soon as the second one had emptied, a wave of pain ripped through her body. But she looked down at her arms and in front of her eyes her skin was tightening and its age spots fading. She felt her back straighten and muscles loosen again. It was worth any amount of pain to be young again – in fact, she decided it was the best pain she'd ever felt.

'I'll take the ones you have in deep freeze, too,' Scary Red said, the rush of feeling young again going to her head.

'I'm sorry. I told you: those vials are The Founder's personal allocation. I can't give them to you.'

'Perhaps you could just check for me, in case there are others? Remember my prescription is from The Founder himself,' Scary Red said, adding a sweetness to her voice.

'I suppose I can take a look,' he said and walked into the back room. Scary Red followed, and as soon as the man entered the deep freeze, she saw her chance and pushed him further inside, then slammed the door shut. He banged on the window, just as Red pressed the 'blast-freeze' button, freezing him solid like a giant lollipop.

She opened the door again and whispered into his ear, 'Chill out, I'll get someone to come and thaw you out later. Maybe.' She looked around and, spotting a silver case of Youth-In-A-Bottle, grabbed it and swept out the door, leaving the man inside.

With every step she felt stronger and more formidable. But she still wasn't content – she wanted to be perfect. And now she had more vials of Youth-In-A-Bottle than she'd ever had before, perhaps she'd go a little bit younger. Just a little bit. What harm could it do?

Chapter 19

Escape at Last!

Completely unaware of Scary Red's return, the kids were celebrating with Bilfred and Wilfred the fact that Anna was safely back from Australia and Ruby was home again.

'Right,' Billy said. 'The village isn't worried about Wilfred any more, Ruby's home safe and Scary Red's on the other side of the world with no chance of getting back, so now we need to find out exactly what's going on in that Terra Nova place.'

'Yeah, I've been thinking,' said Jimmy. 'If those Rangers are the ones taking food to Terra Nova, then they're also our best chance of getting inside to find out what's going on.'

'Hang on, before we do anything, shouldn't we release Bilfred and the rest of the Giants?' said Anna. 'We need a plan.'

'Wait, are you saying we plan before rushing in?' Billy grinned. 'Are you feeling OK?'

Anna stuck her tongue out at him. 'Maybe I've learnt something from you after all,' she said.

'But Scary Red said she'd burn down my garden and hurt all my creature friends if I didn't keep growing,' Bilfred said.

'She's gone, Bilfred,' Anna said reassuringly.

'Besides, you'd still keep growing, so no one at Terra Nova will know any different – it's just that you could come and go as you pleased,' explained Jimmy.

'It's like I said to you before, Bilfred,' said Wilfred. 'You just need a bigger door!'

'I love my garden, but I don't want this wonderful place to be my prison any more. It's my home,' Bilfred said, warming to the idea.

'Bigger doors . . .' Billy said, thinking. 'Wait, that's it! What if we used the sonic blasters the Rangers had to blow holes - I mean *doors* - through the Giants' walls.'

'Great idea!' said Andy.

'You up for this, Bilfred?' Billy asked.

'It would be wonderful, my friends,' the Giant said with a big smile. 'Let's give it a shot!'

'OK, let's go to Scary Red's house and each get a blaster,' said Anna. 'I can get us there in a flash!'

Sonic blasters in hand, the kids lined up in Bilfred's garden.

'Want a bigger door, Bilfred? Then a bigger door it shall be,' Billy said, and took aim with his blaster. He pressed a button and a loud noise came from the weapon . . .

Beeeewwwwwwwwwwww!

Billy went flying about thirty metres in the opposite direction into a compost heap with a puff of dust.

'That wasn't supposed to happen,' he shouted, 'but I'm all right!'

Everyone breathed a sigh of relief, then went to look at the wall. As the dust settled, they saw a Giant-sized hole in the Giant-sized wall.

'Billy, you did it!' shouted Anna with delight.

Bilfred was like a kid at Christmas. He galloped off, jumping and dancing through the hole in the wall.

'FREEDOM! I'm FREEE! I'M FREEEEEEEE!' he shouted, and then, a moment later, he stepped back into the garden and announced: 'I'm home!' Then he jumped back out: 'I'm FREE!' before coming back through the hole and saying: 'But I do like to come home. Anyone for a cup of tea?' Everyone laughed, but agreed it was the perfect time for a tea break.

As they sipped steaming mugs and tucked into pieces of cake, Bilfred said, 'I cannot thank you enough. I cannot believe I'm free.'

'But don't forget we still need you to give the Rangers your fruit and vegetables tonight,' reminded Anna. 'We can't let Terra Nova know what we're up to. Not yet.'

'I think we should wait until every Giant has filled their trunks for the Rangers before we free them all, so we have as much time as possible before anyone notices they're gone,' suggested Jimmy.

'Then we need to blast all the walls, so each and every Giant can leave their gardens if they want to,' said Andy.

'It will be chaos, won't it?' Anna said. 'Hundreds of Giants running around.'

'But it'll be freedom,' Bilfred said with a smile.

'We'll need to speak to them, tell them that we're freeing them, and they might not speak our language – how will we do that?' Billy asked.

'Leave the translating to me,' said Jimmy, who had taken the white cube and was scrolling through the settings. 'There, I think I've solved the problem,' and with a swipe of a finger and twist of the cube, a troop of Rangers whooshed overhead and landed in front of them.

'I've loaded them up with all the languages that the Giants speak, so we'll take a Ranger each and they can communicate for us. Just speak and the Ranger will do the rest.'

'You're brilliant!' Billy beamed.

He pulled out the Sprite map and laid it on the ground, then he took the white cube and projected his map on top of it. It showed the scale of the job they had ahead of them, but, fuelled with Bilfred's tea and cake, nothing was going to stop them. They used the map and cube to divide the gardens up between themselves, making sure every Giant was covered.

'It looks like you might need some help,' said Chief Mirren. 'Let me summon a squadron of Sprites to assist you.'

'Thanks, Chief Mirren!' Billy said gratefully.

'I think we should gather all the Giants in Bilfred's garden, then we can tell them all together about

326

what's happened and our plan,' Jimmy suggested. 'Bilfred had lost his memory when we first found him, so others might have, too. And learning you've been stolen and held prisoner for years is a lot to take in. Being with everyone else might help.'

'At this time of year, I make a bonfire out of woody herbs, because the smoke stops the plants from getting fungus and diseases – it creates really beautiful-smelling billows of smoke. I'll light one today, then the other Giants will see *and* smell where they need to go,' Bilfred said.

As the sun started to set, Billy, Anna, Jimmy and Andy each pulled on a buzzpack, attached a sonic blaster to their arm and flew off, followed by a troop of Sprites and a Ranger. At each garden, they spoke to the Giant and asked if they wanted to be free, before blasting a hole in the wall, and directing them to follow the smoke to Bilfred's garden where they would be told more later.

As Billy flew over the walled gardens, he couldn't help but be amazed by what he saw. Every garden was so different: the way they were laid out, the colours, the types of plants and the unique techniques of each grower. Some grew in the most incredible, wild fashion, some were in perfect order and some were half and half. Where the growers had tried to grow trees on the inside, the Rangers had just increased the height of the wall to prevent escape.

Each Giant seemed to be paired with a garden that matched where they were originally from, so they had the perfect conditions to grow what they knew and

loved from home. They were all dressed differently: some simply wore a pair of shorts; some were almost camouflaged into the surroundings and some were in the brightest colours.

There were Giants from Jamaica, growing peppers, bananas and chillies of all shapes and sizes; there were Japanese Giants, with carefully organized crops of pak choi, beans and square watermelons. The more gardens they found, the more obvious it became that

Scary Red hadn't been stealing random children – she was deliberately trying to ensure the widest food diversity possible, with growers from nearly every continent and country in the world.

Billy couldn't believe these Giants were all once children like him. It was awful that they'd been taken from their families and trapped here.

At his last garden, Billy landed in front of a Tibetan yogi Giant. He was wearing white robes, his face was painted with bright colours and butterflies flew around his head.

Smiling, Billy said through his Ranger, 'Please don't be afraid, I'm here to free you.'

'Free me?' the Giant asked.

'Yes. Have you heard the other blasts? Me and my friends have been freeing trapped Giants in gardens all around you. You're my last one.'

'So, I'm not the only one?' the Giant said, visibly shocked.

'No,' Billy said. 'There are many more. Don't be frightened – they're all just like you. Just follow the smoke and we'll explain more, I promise. Ready?' The

Giant nodded, and, with that, Billy took his stance and blasted a hole through the wall.

'Thank you,' the Giant said to Billy, bowing to him. 'I cannot wait to meet the others.' And he started walking towards the smoke in Bilfred's garden, guided by Billy's Sprite helpers.

Job done, Billy and his support team flew back to meet his friends. As he did so, he saw an electrifying sight: hundreds of Giants heading in the same direction, running, skipping, somersaulting and jumping for joy. The energy fizzing through the woods was only amplified by the joy of nature. It was like everything was vibrating at the same frequency.

But that was nothing compared to the magical sight he saw at Bilfred's garden. The whole Sprite community had gone into overdrive, providing all kinds of incredible food and drink for the confused and excited Giants. They were buzzing everywhere, pouring refreshing drinks into grateful Giant mouths and handing out a buffet of fruit, snacks and biscuits. They were in their absolute element, laughing and joking with the Giants.

Not only that, but also every time a new Giant entered the garden, a Sprite would immediately buddy up with them, staying with them to look after them and keep them company. Billy thought of Balthazar. It had been built for both Sprites and Giants, and, looking at the garden now, the special connection between the two was so obvious.

'Why are they doing that?' asked Andy, bewildered.

'Symbiosis – remember? They pair up because they work better as a team. Like us!' replied Jimmy.

'Oh yeah, I'm definitely better with you guys. Like salt and vinegar crisps,' said Andy.

'That's right, Andy, salt and vinegar crisps,' Jimmy said with a giggle.

'Basil, thank you so much for providing all this wonderful food – it's amazing!' Billy said.

'Oh, it's no's troubles my friend,' the Sprite replied. 'It's the Green Corn full moons tonight, so we weres already goings to be feasting – we've just gots more friends to feed.'

And what a feast it was.

Chapter 20

A Growing Harmony

The kids regrouped around Bilfred's bonfire. 'We did it, guys!' Anna said, proud of what they'd achieved.

'I loved it,' said Jimmy. 'The look on the Giants' faces when they realized they could leave, it was amazing.'

'I know!' said Billy. 'It's one of the best things I've ever done. It makes me so hopeful for the future.' He looked worried for a second. 'But we need to speak to them, to tell them everything that we know and find out what they want to do. But who's going to do that?'

'I think it should be you, Billy – they'll listen to you,' said Anna. 'Go and stand on top of the wall, right there, so all the Giants can see you.' She pointed to a pillar that was raised slightly higher than the wall itself.

'But what do I say?'

'Just speak from the heart – that's when people always listen to you,' she reassured him.

'Thanks, guys. I couldn't do this without you. Will you come and stand with me?'

'Of course we will,' the three chorused. Bilfred lifted them all gently on to the wall.

Billy started to look even more nervous, his fists clenched. 'Will the Giants really hear me?' he asked Jimmy.

'Yes, all the Rangers will come together to translate and amplify your voice, just like they did for Scary Red at Balthazar,' his friend replied, and with another swipe on the cube all but one of the Rangers took positions around the circle of Giants. The final Ranger landed next to Billy.

'GO FOR IT, BILLY!' Andy said. 'You've got this.'

'Giants . . . GIANTS!' Billy shouted, as his voice
reverberated around the Rangers and the walled
garden. 'Please, quiet!'

A hush fell over the Giants. Hundreds of enormous
faces turned to listen to him.

Billy took a deep breath and continued. 'Please

don't worry, you're safe here, we are your friends. I'm Billy, I'm eleven years old, and these are my best human friends, Jimmy, Anna, Andy and Wilfred. This is Bilfred who is a Giant like you, but, also like you, he was once a human and got big! These are our Sprite friends Chief Mirren and Basil, and their Sprite community.' At the mention of Sprites, a ripple of applause went round the Giants, whose faces all broke into huge smiles.

'I've got so much that I need to tell you,' Billy said, his confidence growing with every minute. 'And we will answer all of your questions, but there's no easy way to say the truth . . . You were stolen from your homes as children and brought here to be made prisoners in your gardens. This isn't the world you came from – this is a different one, a long way from home.'

There was a rumbling of anxiety as the truth sank in.

'But it's not all bad news. The evil woman who stole you and trapped you here – Scary Red – has been stopped. We've banished her to a country far away!' All the Giants cheered. 'She works for people in a city called Terra Nova, and we think that's what she's been using your growing skills for, to feed that city somehow. We want to find out what's going on there, but we need your help! You're free to come and go as you please through the holes in your walls, but we still need you to carry on with your great growing like nothing's changed – at least until we can work out how to stop them. It's for everyone's safety. Can you do that for us?'

The Giants all looked at each other and nodded in agreement.

'So, we're asking for you to return to your gardens for now,' Billy continued. 'But every evening, once your daily work is done, you can all come together here, eat delicious food and work out what to do as a family.'

Most of the Giants shouted their support, but one asked: 'What's stopping us from just running away?'

'Nothing. You can leave if you want to, although I'm not sure there's anywhere for you to go here in Waterfall Woods. But we're asking that you help us by staying in your gardens. We think it's the safest place.'

'I know it's scary,' Bilfred added, stepping forward. 'But these children have helped me. You can trust that they will do whatever they can to save us all. Together we are strong, we just need to grow, grow, grow.' Bilfred's voice rang out as he began to sing.

*'So let's get a move on
And grow together,
Show the mud some love
In any kind of weather.
We'll grow, grow, grow
Grow, grow, grow.'*

Suddenly, a voice joined in with him, *'With just a little sun . . .'*

And another shouted, *'And just a little rain!'*

'And just a little love . . .'

'And just a little pain . . .'

Then everyone sang together, *'We'll grow, grow, grow.'*

Tears fell down Bilfred's cheeks. He'd always thought it was his echo in the distance rumbling around the valley that he'd heard as he sang, but now he realized he had been hearing the other Giants joining in his song. It sounded so magical sung by hundreds of voices, the most bizarre and beautiful choir.

As they came to the last part of the song, Bilfred's voice was left singing solo again . . .

'What we've got, we've got each other
Before this day, we had one brother
But we're hundreds now,
And we can help each other out
And we'll grow, grow, grow . . .'

The kids watched in awe from the wall. It was incredible to see all the Giants coming together in song.

'I know we've got work to do,' said Anna. 'But I think I'd like to go home. Seeing all of these Giants without family has made me realize I'm so lucky to have mine.'

'Me too,' said Jimmy.

Andy nodded.

'OK,' Billy said. 'Then, in the morning, come round to mine and we'll go from there.'

Chapter 21

The Fight Back

The next day, the kids reconvened in Billy's kitchen. His mum had made them all crispy smoked bacon and fried egg sandwiches, finished with an all-important blob of HP sauce.

Normally, Billy and Andy could spend ages arguing about the best way to cut a sandwich – diagonally? From top to bottom? Straight across? – but not with this one. They both knew that Billy's mum's oozy egg sandwich was best kept whole to ensure the perfectly cooked fried egg stayed at its finest. And then, when you bit into it, the egg yolk would flood the whole sarnie. Well, usually, unless you had a 'popper', like Andy did that morning! One over-enthusiastic bite sent egg yolk squirting across the table right on to Billy's dad's freshly pressed chinos.

'Oh, for the love of eggs, these chinos are clean on!' he wailed.

'Sorry, Billy's dad!' Andy mumbled, mouth full of sandwich, not looking sorry at all.

'I'm going to have to go and change them,' he grumbled, and went upstairs, leaving the kids alone in the kitchen.

The friends finished off their last mouthfuls, and Andy joyfully licked his plate for any stray bits of yolk

that hadn't embellished Billy's dad's chinos.

'Looks like Wilfred's a local hero,' Billy said, pointing to the headline **MISSING MAN FINDS LOVE** on the front page of the *Little Alverton Journal* that was sitting on the table.

'And Mr Revel kind of has found love, hasn't he?' said Anna. 'Reuniting him with his brother really has been like a romance story.'

'Yeah, we've done a good job there, guys,' said Andy. 'We should be really proud of ourselves.'

'There's a lot we should be proud of,' said Billy. 'We've released the Giants, Bilfred and Wilfred are happy together, and Scary Red's gone, which means we can now concentrate on sorting out the Rhythm and getting to the bottom of what's going on – OUCH!'

'Going on, ouch?' Andy asked, looking confused.

But Billy wasn't paying attention. He looked down at his flint necklace which sizzled with a message from Basil:

HELP! CHIEF MIRREN HAS BEEN CAPTURED BY SCARY RED. COME QUICK! I'M AT HER HOUSE!

'Oh no!' said Anna. 'I can't believe it – how did she get back? Do you think that she could have followed me when I took Ruby home?' She thought of the noises she'd heard when she returned to Bilfred's garden. 'I checked, but I didn't see anything.'

'Even if she did, it's not your fault, Anna,' Billy said. 'We should have known that she wouldn't give up that easily.'

'Billy's right,' Jimmy said. 'She wasn't going to just leave all of this behind without a fight.'

'If anyone's going to hold a grudge, it's her,' said Andy. 'She's got a chip on her shoulder – not that she's eaten one in forever!'

'Come on, let's go,' said Billy determinedly. 'Chief Mirren needs our help. We've got to get rid of Red once and for all.'

Anna used the tetrahedron to transport Billy, Jimmy and Andy immediately to the clearing at Scary Red's house.

Billy spotted Basil just outside. 'Basil! We came as

quickly as we could – where is Chief Mirren?' Billy asked his friend, running towards him.

Basil waved his little arms at Billy and the others. 'Stop! Look out!'

The cackle that followed was unmistakable.

'It shouldn't be this easy,' Scary Red said, gliding seamlessly out of the cover of the trees and over to the kids. 'At last, I have you children exactly where I want you – you have caused me so much trouble. But. Not. For. Much. Longer.'

Billy stared at Scary Red. She looked different. Younger than the last time they'd seen her. Now she looked like she was in her early twenties.

'You don't "have us",' Anna replied fiercely. 'I think you're forgetting I've got your tetrahedron, so what power do you have?'

'Oh, I have more power than you will ever realize,' Scary Red said with a calm spitefulness, her eyes glowing as she stared down at Anna. 'And, in the meantime, I have this itsy bitsy Sprite,' she said, holding up the little cage that was hanging from around her neck like a necklace. 'I believe this is your friend – Chief Mirren,' she said triumphantly. They could see the Sprite squashed into the prison of the pendant, her legs and wings hanging mournfully through the bars.

Basil immediately flew over to sit on Billy's shoulder. 'I'm sorry. I tried to warns yous guys that I thought this was a trap,' Basil started, 'but Scary Red said she would hurt Chief Mirren if I didn't get you here. I'm so sorry.'

'Do not worry about it for another minute,' Billy said, putting a reassuring finger on his friend's back. 'We would always want to come and help.'

'When we get our hands on you, Scary Red, you're not going to know what's hit you!' said Anna.

350

'And what could you do to me?' the woman mockingly asked. 'Push me into another world? Not likely, that childish trick only works once – beginner's luck, shall we say? Anyway, how about a trade? The Sprite for the tetrahedron?' She slipped off the necklace and held it up, letting the small cage swing in the air. Chief Mirren let out a little squeal.

'Don't do it – the tetrahedron is more important than me. Do *not* make the trade! If it's my time, it's my time,' said the chief.

Billy was lost for words – but it didn't matter, because out of nowhere, silhouetted by the cascading rays of the morning sun came a galloping, tumbling, rolling bundle of joy that was Bovine Stinker.

'Beat 'em up, yum-yum!' she shouted.

'Where on earth has she come from?' Billy asked, absolutely amazed. 'And what has she done to her hair?' Billy was right to ask the question, because Bo had done something quite extraordinary – she had made all of the wiry strands on her body stick together into sharp spikes all over her.

Bo ran at full speed towards Red, then, with just

inches to spare before she crashed into her, quickly
rolled herself up, becoming a spiny cannonball,
prickling Scary Red all the way up the back of her
legs. Scary Red screamed and let go of the cage
holding Chief Mirren, giving Bo the time she needed
to grab the necklace before it hit the ground and race
Chief Mirren to safety. Scary Red curled up on the
ground like an upturned beetle and howled in pain,
clutching at her legs.

'Bo! You're our hero,' Jimmy shouted, and the Boona flashed a grin.

'Bo, I can't thank you enough,' Basil said. 'What happened to your hair?'

'Well, when I eat a load of raw potatoes, lots of starchy stuff bubbles out of my mouth, so I spat it in to my hands and twirled it around my hair, turning it into spiky skewers. Great armour, eh?' she replied.

'Genius,' Basil said, as he released Chief Mirren from the cage.

'Guys, how do we get rid of Scary Red?' Anna said to the boys. 'We can't fend her off forever.'

'What we need to do is frighten her enough to leave us alone – you have to stand up to bullies, like I did that time with Bruno,' Billy said.

'How on earth are we going to scare the most frightening lady we've ever met?' said Andy.

'How about if we get her as close to the edge of the waterfall as we can and corner her, then she has to do what we say. We'll promise the Giants will keep producing food – they just can't be prisoners,' Billy replied. 'And that if she wants happy Giants, she needs happy Sprites and children.'

'OK, we're going to need backup for that,' Anna said. 'I'll go to Bilfred's and gather a few Giants to bring back.'

'And all the ammo you can get your hands on,' said Jimmy.

'Got it,' she replied. 'Let's keep in touch on our flints,' and, with that, she quickly created a window and vanished.

'Chief Mirren, Basil, you get out of here, too,' Billy said. 'Go back to Balthazar and rally the other Sprites in case we need extra backup. We'll keep her busy!'

The two Sprites flew off, leaving just Billy, Jimmy, Andy and Bo in the clearing with a now furious Scary Red.

She pressed two bracelets on her wrist, each decorated with blue stones. Sonic booms fired out and the kids scrambled for cover.

'Where's Bo?' Jimmy asked, looking around for the little Boona.

'Beat 'em up, yum-yum! Beat 'em up, yum-yum!'

Bo was once again tumbling and rolling towards

Scary Red, her spikes at the ready!

But this time Scary Red was ready for her, effortlessly snatching the Boona and holding her by the scruff of the neck. Bo arched her back and made a high-pitched sound that echoed around the valley. Scary Red threw the small Boona towards the edge of the trees, where she landed in a dizzy heap.

With Bo dealt with, Scary Red zoned in on the kids again.

'Anna, where are you?' Billy quickly sent over the flint. 'We need you!'

'We're coming. We're just getting some missiles,' Anna replied.

'Where is the girl? Where is my tetrahedron?' Scary Red bellowed.

'OK, guys, it's now or never,' Billy said to Jimmy and Andy. 'Let's give it to her, both barrels!' And he started pulling everything and anything out of his backpack to throw at her – hammers, pliers, winches, paint bombs, whatever he could grab from his supply he passed to the others to throw. But Red's reflexes were super-quick, and she managed to duck and dive from most of them, apart from a couple of paint bombs that thwacked her in the stomach, winding her for a second. It wasn't long before Billy had run out of things to throw.

'You sure you haven't got the kitchen sink in there somewhere?' Andy said.

'Er, no, I don't, wise guy,' Billy replied. 'But I have found the ropes and it's given me an idea – Jimmy, remember when we made a network of tripwires in summer camp? To keep the older boys out of our den? Maybe we can trip up Scary Red, take those powerful shoes off her, then she'll be weaker.'

'Great idea,' said Jimmy. 'Let's do it at the edge of the woods nearest the water. That way we can take the shoes and throw them in the river! We just need some time – Andy, do you think you can keep her occupied close to the house? Do whatever it takes.'

'Course I can – it's lucky you've got me, really,' said Andy, who immediately whipped off his trousers to reveal a pair of Union Jack boxer shorts. 'If this doesn't distract her, nothing will.'

And, with that, Andy started running in all

directions while swinging his trousers around his head, singing Kylie Minogue's 'I Should Be So Lucky' at the top of his lungs. Andy's distraction wasn't stylish, but it was definitely effective. With Scary Red's attention firmly on Andy, Jimmy and Billy darted to the trees to make the network of ropes, which could all be pulled from one central rope to trip her up.

A tear appeared in the air, and finally Anna stepped through with four Giants, each carrying armfuls of giant-sized fruit and veg missiles, including the perfectly named bazooka pumpkins. She took in the sight of Andy running around in his pants being chased by an angry Scary Red.

Spotting her, Andy waved. 'Anna,' he shouted. 'I'm running out of puff, but she doesn't seem tired at all! A little help?'

She didn't need asking twice. 'Give it to 'em, guys!' she shouted to the Giants, and they started firing the food at Scary Red.

'What are you growers doing here?' Scary Red screamed. 'How did you escape from your gardens?'

Giant fruit and veg smashed at her feet, seeds and

gloop flying everywhere. Bilfred had come prepared
with a beedleburp loaded with purple Brussels
sprouts, and he began firing them at her. The Brussels
sprouts might not have finished her off, but they were
highly annoying!

'Andy!' Billy's voice came from the trees. 'Ready!'

Andy pelted towards the area in the woods where

Jimmy and Billy had set their trap, the waterfall thundering in the distance. 'Woo hoo! Bet you can't catch me!' he called back to Scary Red.

Scary Red followed, irritation and rage clouding any good judgement she had – this silly little boy was not going to get the better of her.

It couldn't have been more perfect. She ran straight into the cross-wires that Billy and Jimmy had set up. The boys pulled as hard as they could on all the ropes, tightening them around Red's legs and feet, causing her to trip over. She yelped in frustration, but the more she wriggled, the tighter the ropes became until she was completely caught.

She turned her bracelets towards the ropes, using her blasters to loosen them and untangle herself.

'Oh no,' Billy said to Jimmy. 'I thought the ropes would hold her for a little longer – we're in for it now!'

Billy needn't have worried, because a fresh wave of backup arrived that the kids could never have dreamt of. Bo's high-pitched cry had actually been a Boona emergency signal! The whole Stinker clan had come to fight. There was Mama Boona and the family, the cousins and the cousins' cousins – crowds of burly Boonas, all ready for action.

'Who's been hurting my babies?' Mama Boona bellowed.

'She has,' Billy shouted from behind a tree, pointing at Scary Red, not quite believing they were on the same side for once.

'Right, Boonas, one for all, and all for one – CHARGE!'

A flood of Boonas ran and piled on to Scary Red, completely covering her. Billy took his chance and nipped out from his hiding place to yank off her shoes and remove her bracelets.

'Got 'em!' Billy said triumphantly. He hurled them all as far away as he could and sped off towards the riverbank, hoping to find a place to hide.

Scary Red knew there was no point fighting the Boonas; there were too many. There was only one thing for it, the only thing that would give her the extraordinary hit of energy she needed to escape (not to mention making her even younger) – she wriggled one hand free, reached into the pocket of her dress for a vial and inserted a tube of Youth-In-A-Bottle through the slit in the fabric.

The potion rocketed around her body as it took effect. Once again, pain shot through her, but with it came the strength she needed. With seemingly no effort, she rose up, knocking the Boonas away with ease. They tried to attack her again, but she just kicked, punched and swung every single one of them into the undergrowth, until eventually they ran off, defeated and squealing in pain.

Feeling high on youth and victory, Scary Red leapt up from the ground and scanned her surroundings again, looking for Billy and the others.

Billy's heart raced as he crouched by a rock just next to the river, hoping to stay out of sight. Unfortunately for him the zap of youthful essence had heightened all of Scary Red's senses too, so she spotted him easily. With a horrible grin, she ran at top speed towards him, and before he had a moment to realize what was happening she'd snatched him up by the scruff of his neck like he didn't weigh anything at all.

Her grip was too strong for Billy to break free, no matter how hard he wriggled, and Scary Red carried him into the river. Billy could feel the force of the water around them, but Red strode through it with ease and closer to the waterfall.

'I knew I didn't like the *feel* of your energy – much too good and kind for my liking!' Scary Red snarled. 'Now you'll see what happens when you try to interfere in my plans!' And she held him over the edge of the waterfall.

Billy cried out – was this the end?

Anna, Jimmy and Andy rushed as close as they dared to the riverbank, helplessly staring at Billy and Scary Red. They had to save him!

Anna looked down at the tetrahedron in her hands. The stone was precious, but she had to do something . . .

'Stop! You want this, don't you?' she yelled over the roaring water, holding up the tetrahedron. 'Put. Him. Down!'

Scary Red turned to face Anna. The extra doses of Youth-In-A-Bottle had taken effect and she looked even younger, barely a teenager, but she was still incredibly strong. 'Ah, so you've seen sense. Give me the tetrahedron. Give it to me or . . .' She held Billy closer to the edge.

Anna focused on holding back her tears, not wanting to let Scary Red see how terrified she was. 'If I give you the tetrahedron you'll set Billy free? You promise?' she shouted.

'Of course. Give it to me. Now,' Scary Red yelled impatiently.

By now others from the battle had joined the kids at the waterside and Anna looked around for guidance in the faces of the Giants, Boonas and her best friends. But she knew she didn't have a choice: Billy was worth a hundred tetrahedrons, and everyone else's expressions said the same thing.

'We have to give her what she wants, Anna,' Andy said. 'There's no other way. She's won.'

Then, from out of nowhere, a flying figure appeared in the sky, heading straight for them. It was Grandad! He was being flown through the air by Chief Mirren, Basil and a flurry of Sprites, his right arm pointing in front of him like Superman. They placed him gently in the water, just upstream from Billy and Red.

'Grandad, what are you doing here?' Billy shouted in surprise.

'I've come to stop this evil woman,' Grandad replied, finding his footing in the fast-flowing water. 'Gosh, flying by Sprite is so much fun, now that is first class! And they got me up to speed with what's going on here. Especially you, Scary Red!'

Red laughed. 'And what could an old man

like you do to stop me?'

'More than you think,' he shouted. 'Anna! Throw me that stone.'

Anna did as she was told, tossing the stone to Grandad.

'I'm holding the power now,' he said.

'Actually, I think I'm willing to risk the tetrahedron to get rid of your pesky grandson,' Scary Red said with a snarl. 'So, whatever you might think, I'm the one in charge here.' Her voice was chillingly calm.

'Maybe you would give up the stone, but what about these?' Grandad smiled and opened up his other fist to reveal a handful of vials.

'Where did you get those?' Red asked in shocked confusion. She moved away from the edge and towards Grandad. She let go of Billy, dropping him into the river, and scrabbled around in her pocket – but there was nothing there. She hissed in annoyance as she realized that her remaining vials must have slipped out when she was thrown to the ground back in the clearing.

'That's right,' said Grandad. 'The sprites thought I

should have these. They thought that they might just be important . . . turns out that they were right.'

With Scary Red's attention on the vials and Grandad, Billy took his chance and sprinted away from the edge of the waterfall, and through the thundering water. He scrambled up the bank, reaching his friends, who hugged him tightly – ignoring his soaking-wet clothes. Then they all turned anxiously to watch Grandad's face-off against Scary Red.

'So, now you hand over those vials,' Scary Red said to Grandad. 'And, just so you know, you'll be the first to die when this is over, old man.'

'See, I think that might be the problem. You want to live forever, but I'm not sure you have *actually* lived at all,' Grandad said. 'Me? I've lived a long and happy life filled with the love of friends and family. So, I might be old, but I don't mind because I'm so grateful for what I've had. Getting older is a gift, not a curse. But I don't think you feel like that, do you? You want more, more, more. Nothing is enough, and that means I've got less to lose . . . What are you so scared of?'

Scary Red looked confused. 'There's nothing good

about getting old – you're deluded. Now give me back
my youth,' she demanded.

'Oh, I think you're the one who's deluded,' Grandad
replied. 'But, here, if they mean so much to you, take
them!' He threw the vials at Scary Red, who scrambled
desperately forward to catch them, almost toppling
over in the water, but recovering herself just in time.
She cursed as she watched a couple fall over the
edge of the waterfall, but managed to grab a few.

'Ha! Now, to make myself even stronger and get rid

of you once and for all,' Scary Red said. She looked down at her belly button and inserted a vial.

'Anna! Catch!' Grandad cried, throwing the tetrahedron to Anna. The crystal flew through the air and Anna reached out, grasping it firmly and pulling it back to her chest. And then, before anyone knew what was happening, Grandad raced through the water towards Scary Red. She was so focused on her Youth-In-A-Bottle that she didn't notice him.

'Nooooo!' Billy cried as he realized what was happening. It was like watching everything in slow motion as Grandad launched himself at the distracted Scary Red, pushing her over the edge of the waterfall.

'I LOVE YOU, BILLY!' Grandad's cry came, as the two figures flew out of sight.

Billy rushed down the bank, closer to the edge of the waterfall, and peered down, leaning as far as he could without risking falling himself. There was nothing. No Grandad. No Scary Red. Just the rush of water as it fell to the river below.

Chapter 22

End of an Era

Everyone searched for Grandad for hours. The kids used their buzzpacks to fly up and down the river and the Giants and Boonas walked up and down the water's edge. Chief Mirren, Basil and the Sprites instantly jumped into action, flitting here and there, looking through the bushes on the banks and diving into the water to see if there was any sign of the old man.

But there was nothing. How could anything survive plunging into that roaring torrent? The water was just too strong.

As it grew dark, the kids, Basil and Chief Mirren gathered together again in the clearing by Red's

house and sat in a silent circle.

'Just think of the good times, Billy,' Anna suggested, gently rubbing her friend's back.

'But it hurts,' Billy cried. 'I loved him so much.'

'There's only one way to love and that's with a full heart,' Chief Mirren said gently. 'Yes, you're hurting right now, but because you loved him so hard, your grandad knew right till the very end that you loved the bones of him, Billy, and that's all he'd ever want. I know it's hard, but you have to remember the good times . . .'

Billy closed his eyes and breathed deeply. 'I had
so many magical times with my grandad. He was the
best. He was always there at sports days, cheering me
on, even when I was last; he was the one who taught
me how to ride a bike, though I might have run over
his toes a few times.' A smile twitched at the corners
of Billy's mouth as he remembered, and everyone
chuckled, too. 'He sat with me making Lego – our
Black Monarch's Castle is still up in my bedroom; then
there were the cinema trips where we'd have to have
sweet popcorn because it was his favourite. He was
the one who taught me how to wire a plug and use a
soldering iron, not to mention how to make the best
porridge in the whole wide world . . .' Billy tailed off at
the thought, tears streaming down his face. He
couldn't believe his lovely Grandad was just . . . gone.

Anna put a comforting arm around Billy. 'Your
grandad saved us, Billy. He was so brave. He gave up
his life for us because he loved us so much. And he
knew how much you loved him – you told him every
time you saw him.'

Basil flitted over and just hugged Billy's nose. 'I'm

371

not lettings go, Billy,' he said. 'I don't knows what else to do.'

'To be honest, he's probably saved so much more, well beyond us,' said Jimmy. 'He stopped Scary Red for good. Which means that she won't be able to take any more children to use as growers.'

'Your grandad is a hero,' said Andy, tears running down his cheeks. 'I'll never forget him.'

But none of their words helped. Billy didn't want his grandad to be a hero, he wanted him to be there.

'Billy, I feel your pain,' said Chief Mirren, sitting gently on his shoulder. 'My grandpa died saving my life in the great battle of Balthazar. Your grandad was a very wise man, and with wisdom comes selflessness and an acceptance that you would give anything for the people you love. Even if that's your life. He was very special. Some souls leave behind a trail of light and love that is never to be forgotten.'

Chief Mirren crossed her hands, interlocked her thumbs and wiggled her fingers to make the shape of a flying butterfly, then hundreds of Sprites did exactly the same and hummed together – a note that somehow seemed to comfort and lighten the atmosphere all at the same time, vibrating through every living thing. It was the most beautiful noise.

Chief Mirren continued, 'Your grandad is flying now, and will become part of the Rhythm soon.' She gave Billy a warm smile. 'The destination is the same for all good souls.'

'Thank you, Chief Mirren,' Billy replied and smiled back weakly.

Things went by in a dizzy blur for Billy. He knew his friends were talking to him, telling him they should go home and tell his parents what had happened, saying goodbye to the Sprites, Giants and Boonas, but he was so numb that it was as if he was underwater: he couldn't hear or feel anything.

By the time they reached the Green Giant pub, he had no real memory of how he'd got home.

'OK, breathe, Billy, deep breaths,' Anna said to him. 'We're all here for you. What do you want to do?'

Billy looked at his three best friends. 'I think I have to tell my parents. Everything.'

'Everything?' said Jimmy, looking worried.

'Yeah, everything,' replied Billy.

'No, you can't do that, Billy,' Anna said. 'Tell them about your grandad, yes, but not the woods. Don't forget what happened to Wilfred when he told the truth – he was an outcast for years and years. We twinky promised we'd never tell. It's too dangerous!' She held out her little finger. 'Twinky promise again.' Reluctantly, Billy interlocked his finger with hers, and Jimmy and

Andy joined in. 'You know it makes sense, Billy,' Anna said. He nodded.

Billy walked into the pub and to the flat upstairs – it was early evening, so he knew his mum would be in the flat having tea while his dad was at Wednesday football. His friends followed just behind in an uneasy silence, worried about what would happen next.

'Billy!' said his mum as he pushed open the door to the flat. 'Is that you, Billy? You won't believe the day I'm having . . .'

Then, as she saw his tear-stained face, she said, 'Billy, you all right? Whatever's the matter?'

Billy took a deep breath as his chin dropped to his chest. 'It's Grandad. He's gone . . .'

'Gone mad, I can tell you that much,' his mum said crossly. 'He ran out of here this morning when you weren't home – I've never seen him move so fast.'

Then he raised his head and looked her in the eyes: 'No, Mum, he's *gone* gone . . .'

'I know! Gone crazy! Honestly, I don't know what's the matter with him . . .'

'Mum, you're not listening to me!' Billy shouted.

'I'm trying to tell you Grandad is dead!'

Mum's face froze for a second, then she threw both hands on to her hips and said, 'Yeah, and I'm trying to tell you he's dead naughty – I've had to put him in your old naughty corner for making all this mess. Look!' She stepped aside to reveal Grandad, dripping wet, sitting on a chair in the corner of the living room, holding a bundle of red rags.

Grandad looked at the kids sheepishly and gave them a wave. Billy and the others gasped in disbelief. How was it possible that Grandad was here? They'd seen him topple over the edge and disappear, hadn't they? How could this be?

'Grandad! You're . . . alive?' Billy said in shock and amazement. 'This is the happiest day of my life!'

'Yep, alive and dripping!' his mum replied. Grandad gave a guilty smile. 'Right, kids, settle down – you go and have a chat with Grandad and work out how he's come back from the dead.' She rolled her eyes at her son's dramatic entrance. 'I've got to phone the police constable.'

'What about?' Billy asked, wiping his eyes.

'Your grandad will explain,' she replied as she walked into the kitchen.

Billy looked at his friends, whose faces were as shocked as his.

'You don't think your mum is phoning the police because Grandad told her what happened, do you?' said Anna, fearing the worst.

She was relieved Billy's grandad was OK, but what if he'd spilled all the secrets he'd discovered over the last few days?

'Grandad wouldn't do that!' Billy said. 'Come on – he'll tell us himself.' He ran over to give him the biggest hug.

'Careful,' Grandad said, putting his arms out to stop him. 'Slow down, Billy, slow down. Gently now, come and have a look.' He put his arms out to show them what was wrapped up inside the rags.

Four heads peered in. A tiny baby lay in Grandad's arms. Then Billy let out a gasp as he noticed a big blue ring on the baby's nose . . .

'Wow, no way!' whispered Billy, pointing it out to the others.

'What?' Jimmy said. 'Does that mean . . .?'

'It's Scary Red!' finished Anna. 'But how?'

'I don't know quite what happened,' Grandad said in a hushed whisper. 'Maybe whatever stuff she took reacted with the water or something? I never let go, even when we got churned up by the waterfall, and when I came up for air, Scary Red the adult was gone, and this baby was in my hands. Eventually, I managed to pull both of us to the banks, and I was so far away and lost that I decided to just start walking. I began to recognize bits of the woods, and I made my way back to the oak tree that got hit by lightning and came back here.'

The kids didn't know what to say. They stared at the small, beautiful, perfect, helpless baby, unable to believe it was the same person as the evil red lady!

'I think we need to look after her,' Grandad said.

'Really? Why? She's evil,' said Jimmy.

'I don't know if anyone can be *born* evil,' Grandad said. 'I think there was something that happened to her in her old life that turned her rotten. Was it nature: she was born like that? Or nurture: she was poisoned

by the things she was taught and experienced?'

The first one to dive in was Andy. 'I don't think anyone is born that evil either – it's got to be nurture.'

'Yep, I think so too,' agreed Anna.

'And me,' said Billy.

But Jimmy hesitated. 'Hmmm. Animals are born with traits to survive and to hunt and to steal – survival of the fittest. So maybe for me it's got to be a bit of both.'

'Whatever it is,' Grandad said, 'all I know is I've got a little baby in my arms now and that's like a fresh start. And I think perhaps we should try to keep her near to us – you know what they say: keep your friends close and your enemies closer. We don't want to risk that Terra Nova place finding her.'

'OK, so we need to work out a plan,' said Billy. 'Good thing you've got some experts in that on your side, Grandad.' He smiled at his friends.

'Well, how about it wasn't just *you* that found the baby,' suggested Anna. 'If I was with you, then perhaps I could tell my parents that I don't want her to go anywhere else, and they could apply to foster the baby. My mum and dad are the kindest people and have fostered lots of kids. We've got a really good chance of keeping Red under our watch if she's my little sister.'

Grandad nodded in agreement. 'That sounds like a good idea, Anna.'

'Are we forgetting that she's a child snatcher? That she wanted to kill Billy?' Jimmy asked. 'Do you really want her living in your house, Anna?'

As if on cue, Baby Red gurgled sweetly and smiled at them. 'She *WAS* a child snatcher, but is she the same person now?' asked Anna. 'Perhaps Grandad's right – this is a fresh start and she's started again. She's hardly a threat now. Most people deserve a second chance.'

'It's like rebooting your ZX Spectrum, Jimmy,' Billy said. 'When your games machine starts glitching, what do you do?'

'I turn it off and on again,' said Jimmy.

'Exactly! And that's what's happened with Red,' said Anna. 'I feel like we should drop the "Scary" part now, don't you?'

Jimmy thought for a moment. 'Maybe that makes sense. And I suppose we shouldn't just give up on a person without even giving them a chance to change. No matter how scary they were.'

'So, we're all in?' Grandad asked. 'We'll have to give it one hundred per cent, though. Whatever you do in life, you should give one hundred per cent – unless you're giving blood, then it's not a good idea.'

Billy, Anna, Jimmy and Andy nodded and giggled.

'But, if we do this, we can never tell anyone else the truth about Red,' Grandad said, his face serious. 'Agreed?'

Billy held out his little finger and the others grabbed hold of it. 'Twinky promise,' they all said in unison.

'How did you even know where we were?' Billy asked his grandfather. 'Your timing was immaculate!'

'I came to see you at your mum's this morning, but when she told me that you'd all run off, I knew something bad must've happened in the woods, so I headed straight there and hugged the oak tree. There I hailed Chief Mirren, Basil and a flurry of Sprites who were dashing through the forest to help you guys and hitched a lift. Easy! Lovely creatures, aren't they?' he replied.

'Well, I'm so glad you came,' Billy said. 'Even if you did give me the fright of my life.' He hugged Grandad with all his might.

When Billy let go, he looked at the small baby in his grandad's arms. He'd seen so many weird and

wonderful things since they first discovered the truth
about Waterfall Woods, but this was without doubt the
weirdest and most wonderful yet.

As the baby smiled, he felt a flutter of hope.
For now, with Red transformed and the tetrahedron
safely with Anna, he hoped Terra Nova would have
no way of stealing any more children to trap in
their walled gardens. And with the Giants now free,
too, at least some of the past wrongs had been
put right.

Billy's mum came bustling back into the room.

'Right, kids I need some privacy up here. The police are coming round to interview Grandad. So, you go downstairs and have something delicious to eat – actually, your dad's been trying out a new special, Billy, so I'm sure he could do with your feedback. I've eaten it too many times! He's on version thirteen, so this could be your lucky dinner,' she said to them with a wink.

'What is it, Mum?' Billy asked, hoping it was going to be a big hug of a meal, as he'd been through so much.

'Chicken Kyiv with crispy bacon bits and cheesy broccoli mash,' his mum replied. 'You're gonna love it!'

Billy's dad had just got back from football and was still in his kit in the pub kitchen. 'Ah, kids! Are you ready for a taste sensation?' he asked. 'This is one of the tastiest dishes ever – it's chicken, wrapped in crispy breadcrumbs, stuffed with garlic butter and nuggets of crispy bacon, so that when you cut into it it's going to squirt everywhere and make you very happy!' The smile on his face was infectious!

'Does that come with chips, Mr Palmer?' Andy asked, hoping upon hope.

'Ah, no, it's cheesy broccoli mash and baby spinach,' Billy's dad replied.

'Delicious!' said Andy, who had never come across a food he didn't like.

'And you can have my new favourite fizzy drink – Appletise. Right, who's up for it?'

The kids all cheered and tucked into the most gorgeous dinner.

'Gosh, I needed that,' said Jimmy afterwards. 'Your dad does the best grub, Billy!'

'I know,' said Billy. 'He's the greatest.'

'How about some pudding, kids?' Billy's dad called.

'There's always room for pudding, Mr Palmer!' Anna said, the boys furiously nodding in agreement. 'What is it?'

'Caramelized banana sticky toffee pudding. Soft, spongy, sticky goodness with an oozy pool of melting vanilla ice cream – sound good?'

The kids all cheered.

As his dad dished out dessert, Billy looked around

at his friends tucking in and chatting excitedly with each other. They'd all been through some incredible things together, and he was so glad to have had his best friends by his side through it all.

But even though they'd stopped Scary Red and freed the trapped Giants, Billy knew Waterfall Woods wasn't out of danger – and neither was their own world. The Myas' message had been clear: the Rhythm was in trouble still, and it was because of Terra Nova.

The city was still a mystery, so there was more investigating to be done. They had to go back to the woods, discover a way to get inside and learn the truth.

He thought of the brilliant blue stone that he'd taken from Scary Red's house, which was still sitting in his backpack. Billy didn't really know why he'd taken it or why he wanted to keep it a secret. But he had a feeling that the stone and the power it held was somehow the key to helping the Rhythm. If only he could work out how to harness that power . . .

'Come on, Billy, tuck in!' his dad said, shaking Billy from his thoughts.

Billy smiled. The adventure might not be over yet. But, for now, there was so much to celebrate – for a start his grandad was safe, he had the most brilliant friends, and the Giants were happy. Grinning wider, he plunged his spoon into the steaming hot sponge and thought, *This is how every adventure should end.*

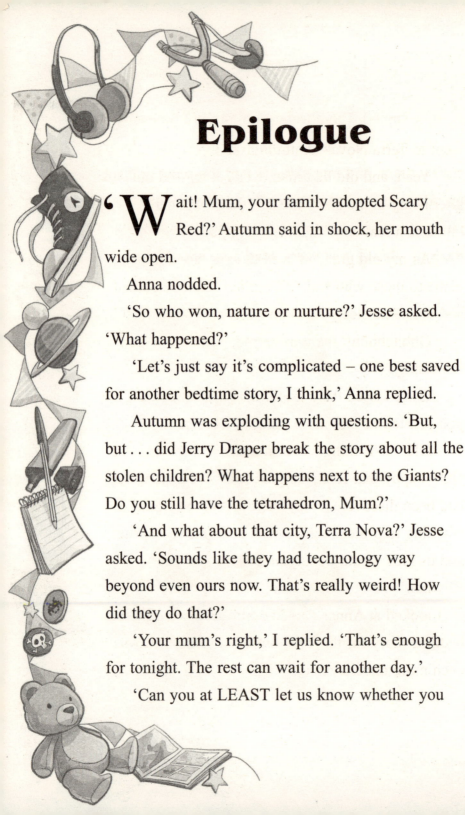

Epilogue

'Wait! Mum, your family adopted Scary Red?' Autumn said in shock, her mouth wide open.

Anna nodded.

'So who won, nature or nurture?' Jesse asked. 'What happened?'

'Let's just say it's complicated – one best saved for another bedtime story, I think,' Anna replied.

Autumn was exploding with questions. 'But, but . . . did Jerry Draper break the story about all the stolen children? What happens next to the Giants? Do you still have the tetrahedron, Mum?'

'And what about that city, Terra Nova?' Jesse asked. 'Sounds like they had technology way beyond even ours now. That's really weird! How did they do that?'

'Your mum's right,' I replied. 'That's enough for tonight. The rest can wait for another day.'

'Can you at LEAST let us know whether you

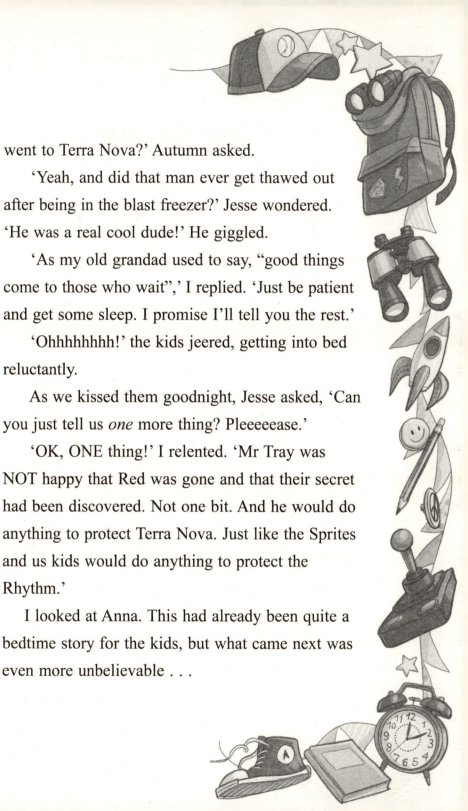

went to Terra Nova?' Autumn asked.

'Yeah, and did that man ever get thawed out after being in the blast freezer?' Jesse wondered. 'He was a real cool dude!' He giggled.

'As my old grandad used to say, "good things come to those who wait",' I replied. 'Just be patient and get some sleep. I promise I'll tell you the rest.'

'Ohhhhhhhh!' the kids jeered, getting into bed reluctantly.

As we kissed them goodnight, Jesse asked, 'Can you just tell us *one* more thing? Pleeeeease.'

'OK, ONE thing!' I relented. 'Mr Tray was NOT happy that Red was gone and that their secret had been discovered. Not one bit. And he would do anything to protect Terra Nova. Just like the Sprites and us kids would do anything to protect the Rhythm.'

I looked at Anna. This had already been quite a bedtime story for the kids, but what came next was even more unbelievable . . .

Thank You!

Well, here it is! My second children's fiction book – a continuation of the magic Waterfall Woods legend. And it's been another epic journey for me. I've used a different technique to write this one (it didn't take me four years!), but I've had so much fun with it, and my confidence has grown, as well as my love of storytelling – who would've thought?!

What's made me so very happy has been seeing how much joy kids have got from reading *Billy and the Giant Adventure* – and hearing it on audiobook! And, in the same way, I want this book to not just be a rip-roaring ride – which it absolutely is! – but also to help teach young people some lessons I've learned in my life. About being kind, being a good friend, always being open to giving people second chances, and finding your own way/place in the world.

OK, so many people to thank. Of course, family comes first – Mum and Dad x; Jools, Poppy, Daisy, Petal, Buddy and River – you inspire me every day. To Paul Quinton, thank you so much for your time and head space.

This time around, unconventionally, I've shared my writing process with some brilliant young readers, just to keep me on the straight and narrow! Honestly, their feedback has been really useful and helped me shape the book, so a great big thank you to eight-year-old Monty Bell, eight-year-old Fergus Sweet and nine-year-old Zara Murrell.

I want to thank my JO HQ team. My brilliant editors Rebecca Morten and Rebecca Verity. We've had some fun doing this, haven't we?! To my brilliant creative team James Verity and

Barnaby Purdy. Big ups to my marketing and PR teams, Tamsyn Zietsman, Rosalind Godber, Michelle Dam and Ashleigh Bishop. To Louise Holland, Zoe Collins and Sean Moxhay for their continued support and belief – and special thanks to the ever-patient Ali Solway. You the best!

To my brilliant Puffin team – Jane Griffiths, my excellent editor (we'll get those extra farts in another book) and Ben Hughes, my brilliant designer who has delivered once again! Then to the wider team: Tania Vian-Smith and Phoebe Williams; Lottie Halstead and Hannah Sidorjak; Kat Baker and the wonderful UK and International Sales teams; Alice Grigg and the whole of Rights. And, of course, Francesca Dow, MD.

To the brilliant illustrator Mónica Armiño – once again you've pulled it out of the bag! What gorgeous illustrations.

I've had the pleasure of making another brilliant audiobook. Thank you to James Keyte, Chris Thompson and Roy McMillan (we love you, Roy!) at Penguin Random House Audio, then my favourites at Vaudeville Sound: Dan Jones, Kate 'Bronzie' Bronze, Luke Hatfield, Enzo Cannatella, Lois Green, Zack Marshall and Sophie McGuire. And special shout-outs to the actors who brought it all to life: Dexter Fletcher, Jason Flemyng, Amy Wren, Kadeem Ramsay, Benny Mails and Tamzene Allison-Power. This time around we've also worked with the brilliant Mark Strong, the unbeatable Alfie Boe and the beautiful Beth Dillon – it's so great to have you on board! Last but not least, a huge thanks to Tobie Tripp and Daniel Moyler for bringing all the music.

BIG LOVE!
Jamie O xxx

Read on for some AMAZING recipes from Jamie Oliver, inspired by Billy's adventure!

These recipes are designed to be made together, so while we hope you have fun cooking up a storm, always make sure you have a grown-up to help you in the kitchen and be very careful around knives and hot ovens.

For nutrition advice and lots more, visit jamieoliver.com/billy.

Bilfred's garden soup

with lovely veg, beans, grains and potato dumplings

Serves 8

Total time: 50 minutes

2 cloves of garlic

2 small onions

2 fresh bay leaves

olive oil

2 carrots

2 sticks of celery or 1 leek

600g mixed green veg, such as courgettes, fennel, chard, tenderstem broccoli, asparagus, kale, peas, broad beans

1 vegetable stock cube

1 x 400g tin of quality plum tomatoes

2 x 400g tins of beans, such as cannellini, butter, haricot

100g random dried pasta or rice

400g potato gnocchi

Parmesan cheese or pesto, to serve

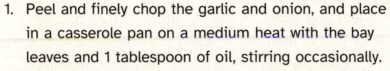

1. Peel and finely chop the garlic and onion, and place in a casserole pan on a medium heat with the bay leaves and 1 tablespoon of oil, stirring occasionally.

2. Peel the carrots, trim the celery or leek, then finely chop them, adding to the pan as you go. Cook for 10 minutes, or until softened, stirring regularly.

3. Meanwhile, prep your green veg, chopping courgettes and fennel into ½cm chunks and finely slicing broccoli, asparagus, chard and kale.

4. Crumble the stock cube into the pan, add a good pinch of black pepper and the tinned tomatoes, breaking them up with your spoon. Swirl some water around the tin and pour it in, followed by the beans, juice and all.

5. Pour in 800ml of water, bring to the boil, then add the pasta or rice and the green veg. Cover and simmer for 10 to 15 minutes, or until the pasta or rice is just cooked, stirring occasionally and adding splashes of water if needed. Gently add the gnocchi for the last few minutes to give you little dumplings.

6. Season the soup to perfection, then divide between your bowls. Nice with a grating of Parmesan cheese or a dollop of pesto to finish.

Optional smoky extra

To make Bilfred's smoke float, find yourself a little metal bowl that you can float in the soup after you've added the green veg. Pop a small slice of unsalted butter into the bowl, tear in 4 sprigs of woody herbs, such as rosemary, sage or thyme, then ask an adult to carefully set fire to the herbs. Cover the pan with a lid for the rest of the time, letting the herbs impart a wonderfully smoky flavour into the butter. Once the soup is done, carefully remove the metal bowl (it will be very hot!), serve up the soup, then pour a little smoky butter over each portion.

Andy's special cheese toastie
with bonus tomato ketchup and crisps!

Serves 1
Total time: 10 minutes

soft unsalted butter

2 slices of wholemeal bread or white bloomer

30g melty cheese, such as Cheddar, Red Leicester, Emmental

optional: a little blue cheese

tomato ketchup

optional: a few of your favourite crisps

1. Lightly butter the bread on both sides.
2. Grate or slice the melty cheese, then sprinkle it across one piece of bread, and crumble the blue cheese on top, if using.
3. Add some splodges of ketchup and a few crisps, if you like a bit of crunch. Andy goes for beef and onion, but feel free to use your own favourite flavour; then place the other piece of buttered bread on top.

4. Now, either place the sandwich in a hot toastie machine for 7 minutes, or put it in a sturdy non-stick frying pan on a medium-low heat, placing something flat with a little weight on top of the sandwich, before toasting for 2 minutes on each side, or until golden and crisp.

5. Slice and serve, or wrap in tinfoil if you want to take it out on the go with you. Delicious with some crunchy veg sticks like cucumber, carrot or pepper on the side.

Brilliant banana sticky toffee pud

soft, spongy, sticky goodness served with ice cream

Serves 10

Total time: 50 minutes

200g pitted Medjool dates

175g unsalted butter, plus extra for greasing

75g golden syrup

2 ripe bananas

150g light brown sugar

2 large free-range eggs

150g self-raising flour

75ml single cream

1. Preheat the oven to 180°C. Boil the kettle. In a small jug, cover the dates with 150ml of boiling kettle water, making sure they're submerged.

2. Grease a 20cm x 20cm square baking tin and line with greaseproof paper. Pour in the golden syrup, making sure it covers the base, then dot over 25g of butter.

3. Peel the bananas, slice into rounds and arrange in a single layer over the syrup and butter, then set aside.

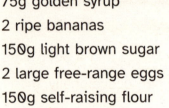

4. Pour the dates and soaking water into a food processor, add 75g each of butter and sugar and blitz until combined, then crack in the eggs, add the flour and blitz again.

5. Gently pour the mixture into the tin over the bananas, then bake for 35 minutes, or until golden and an inserted skewer comes out clean.

6. To make a sauce, put the remaining 75g each of butter and sugar and the cream into a small pan and simmer until slightly thickened and a deep gold in colour, gently swirling the pan occasionally, then pour into a serving jug.

7. Carefully turn out the pud on to a nice board or serving platter and peel away the greaseproof paper to reveal the sticky bananas. Slice and serve warm with ice cream and a drizzle of the sauce.

Mix it up

You could try using sliced apples or pears in place of the bananas!

Jamie Oliver

is a global phenomenon in food and campaigning. He has sold over 50 million books worldwide. He started cooking at his parents' pub (the inspiration for the Green Giant in this book!) at the age of eight in Essex. After leaving school he began a career as a chef that took him to the River Café, where he was spotted by a television production company and the Naked Chef was born. Jamie now lives in Essex with his wife Jools and their five children.

Mónica Armiño

is a Spanish illustrator. She graduated in Fine Arts and is based in Madrid. She has published several books with various publishers and agencies in Europe and the USA. Mónica also works in the animation industry as a character designer, background artist and colour and texture artist for feature films and pre-school TV series like the award-winning *Puffin Rock*.

Don't miss the briliant audio editions of Billy's adventures!

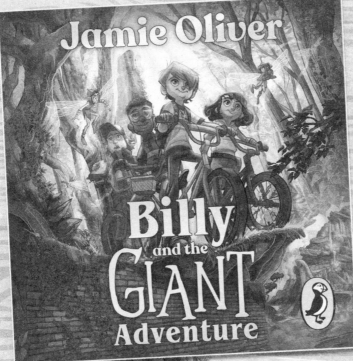

Jamie Oliver

Billy
and the
GIANT
Adventure

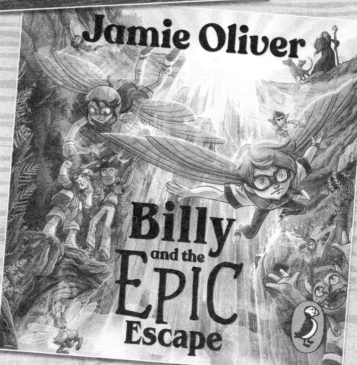

Jamie Oliver

Billy
and the
EPIC
Escape

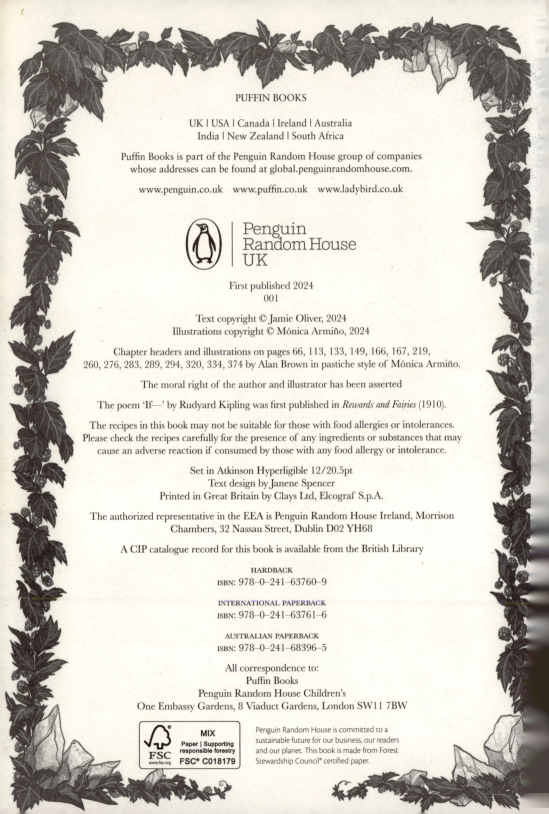

PUFFIN BOOKS

UK | USA | Canada | Ireland | Australia
India | New Zealand | South Africa

Puffin Books is part of the Penguin Random House group of companies
whose addresses can be found at global.penguinrandomhouse.com.

www.penguin.co.uk   www.puffin.co.uk   www.ladybird.co.uk

Penguin
Random House
UK

First published 2024
001

Set in Atkinson Hyperligible 12/20.5pt
Text design by Janene Spencer
Printed in Great Britain by Clays Ltd, Elcograf S.p.A.

The authorized representative in the EEA is Penguin Random House Ireland, Morrison
Chambers, 32 Nassau Street, Dublin D02 YH68

A CIP catalogue record for this book is available from the British Library

HARDBACK
ISBN: 978–0–241–63760–9

INTERNATIONAL PAPERBACK
ISBN: 978–0–241–63761–6

AUSTRALIAN PAPERBACK
ISBN: 978–0–241–68396–5

All correspondence to:
Puffin Books
Penguin Random House Children's
One Embassy Gardens, 8 Viaduct Gardens, London SW11 7BW